Life on the Edge

Vera Morrill

Published by New Generation Publishing in 2013

First Edition

www.newgeneration-publishing.com

 New Generation Publishing

ABOUT THE AUTHOR

VERA MORRILL, formerly an English teacher, holds an Hons. Degree from Southampton University. A former English examiner on the Cambridge University Examination Board, she is a Licentiate of the London Academy of Music & Dramatic Art, with a Teaching Diploma for Speech and Drama and a Gold Medal for acting. She has written and broadcast stories for the BBC, scripted and produced theatrical productions and is a published poet.

For all my loved ones

In 'Life on the Edge' a modern travel escort uses the 14th Century Chaucer's idea from 'The Canterbury Tales' where, at the end of each day the pilgrims stopped at a tavern for food and rest. Realising that the long evening hours would pass more quickly if they entertained each other by telling stories, they soon found that, through the stories, although meeting as strangers, they had learned a great deal about each other. Here a modern group of tourists have also met as strangers. Now they are faced with the most extreme and terrifying circumstances. Will the same idea help them to bond and become mutually supportive? Their guide decides it is worth a try, but will they co-operate?

Prologue

Hazel gazed out at the rolling Yorkshire moors, thickly blanketed with snow.

How dare people say life begins below the Watford Gap? Yorkshire's such a beautiful county with so many delights to offer and the pristine snow coming every winter without fail, always adds to its breathtaking charms. Fingers crossed, its early arrival won't play havoc with my arrangements for New Year.

Christmas, thank God, is over. Christmas alone is, without a doubt, the most bitter of pills to swallow. Stupid to decorate when the likelihood of anyone crossing one's threshold is zero.

Turning to look back into the room Hazel grimaced. As always she had made a token effort. The fireplace had once again held its artificial spray of holly and ivy, the mini fir tree with its tiny baubles had sparkled on top of the book shelves and the vase of red silk roses had held pride of place in the centre of the small dining table with her few cards scattered around. Within the last few minutes the decorations had been packed away, the cards removed and now, suddenly, the room seemed strangely bare.

She'd watched the inevitable replaying of TV films – decided she now knew the words of 'She wore a yellow ribbon' by heart. As always, wept a few tears hearing the silver-toned voice of the choir boy singing 'Once in Royal David's City' initiating the choral feast at King's College, Cambridge, and listened intently to the Queen's speech.

Her photo album and box of snaps were brought out on Boxing Day. This was Memory Lane time. Twenty years ago, she and her sister sliding down a snow-covered hill on a toboggan, with their parents standing at the bottom of the slope. Sister Judy, now safely ensconced in a remote part of Scotland, making it impossible to come south and assist whenever the parents reached the point of needing help. Crying effectively at their funerals, but never offering assistance. The parents on holiday, bless them, frozen in time. Mum, pint-sized, with a shock of dark auburn hair and Dad, hair receding, eyes twinkling and his specs clipped to the front of his sweater.

The first photo of herself and Len, two silly infatuated youngsters. She, like Mum on the small side, he, almost six feet and looking rather bashful. Their wedding photo, already dated after just nine years, the snap of them sitting on a low wall on the moors, looking as if they wished they were far away from their surroundings and each other. She'd never been quite sure exactly when the rot set in, when she'd first realised that they were totally unsuited as a couple. Len's qualification as an accountant had turned him into what her Dad had called 'a bean counter', almost immune to creativity and after a while almost humourless.

Her own job in a travel agent's, started after leaving school, Len regarded as something requiring little or no brains. Yes, he was well aware that she had long ago progressed beyond the general dogsbody duties, making tea etc., but he'd never seemed to acknowledge that. In the fourth year of their marriage she had progressed to a senior customer assistant with the relevant diplomas and had been required to go overseas often to assess holiday sites, so as to be able to discuss with conviction the assets or otherwise of destinations required. His comments regarding 'looking for adjacent building sites' and 'grubby duvets' just about summed up the amount of respect he had for the work she was doing.

Her return from one of those trips to find him gone

and a note saying they had obviously come to the end of the road, neither shocked nor disappointed her – in fact her strongest emotion was one of overwhelming relief. Now she could get on with her life.

The separation had left her with enough money to purchase her flat, specially chosen at second floor level so that she could both feel safe and enjoy the view. At the same time she started to explore the possibility of working as a travel guide for overseas holiday groups and increasing her language skills. The question of another permanent relationship was shelved – there were, she felt sure, exciting places to visit and explore. She was just thirty, men could wait!

Now, with Christmas behind her, she was faced with the prospect of her second visit to Madeira for the New Year break, the highlight of which would be the world famous fireworks display on New Year's Eve. Her bag was packed and all her documentation, the flat was cleared of anything which might go stale and it was time to set the alarm and get to bed, in preparation for an early morning start.

Unbelievably, she was looking forward to it. The package had changed everything! Arriving the day before Christmas Eve, obviously from her boss at the Head Office of the travel company, she had put it on one side until the evening of Boxing Day. Deliberately! It probably contained the usual petty list of complaints, with advice about what she should and shouldn't do in Madeira. It could wait! When finally read, its contents had in fact surprised and exhilarated her. At last, something different, something to get her teeth into. Now, instead of dreading the next day, she could anticipate it with delight. It promised new ventures, a secret for her to keep and good news to impart, that should make even the dullest of travellers come out of their shells and sit up and take notice.

As today's youngsters would say 'Bring it on'!

***

Chapter 1

I should be used to it by now, but oh dear! Hazel, smile fixed firmly in place, surveyed the assembled group around her. *Anyone would think we were going to the outer reaches of Mongolia, one or two look downright terrified. Wait until they know what I know!*

"I can't stress strongly enough that you are allowed only one piece of hand luggage. And yes, ladies, that does include handbags." Murmurs from the ranks.

"You were warned at the check-in counter and on your holiday booking forms. If anyone has two pieces then you must try and put one inside the other and," pre-empting the groans from one or two of the women, "Yes, I'm afraid that does mean forcing handbags into holdalls or small cases, otherwise they will be confiscated until we return."

As some of them proceeded to do just that, Hazel fumed inwardly. *Why didn't people listen to the news or read the papers and make themselves aware of what's happening in the big wide world?* At last they were all upright, making eye contact and looking at her expectantly. Smile once again in place, Hazel said, "Have your boarding passes ready please and try and sit together in the departure lounge, it will make life easier."

Fat chance of getting 14 seats in close proximity, she thought. I'll just have to make contact with some and leave the others for on the flight. At least it looks as if we'll be leaving on time.

"Please follow me everyone, our departure gate is No.25." Purposefully striding forward, Hazel quickly glanced over her shoulder to ensure they were all doing just that. The young couple at the rear of the group looked totally confused, but were at least following the others. She heard the moans and groans when they were confronted with yet another corridor and then another walkway and heard the sighs of relief as those in front spotted the No. 25 sign up ahead. Gathering them again into a group, she grumbled to herself again…*Why were there thirteen when she had been quite explicit to the Primetime people that she was only prepared to take 10 maximum? I'm not overly superstitious, but thirteen! If that isn't asking for trouble. O.K. so, with me, it's 14, but after I'd specifically asked…! Until that letter yesterday, I was all set to tell them what to do with their job, but now…*

Hazel's first point of contact was with the Williams, a couple in their forties. She, rather plump and flamboyant, her smaller husband seeming permanently in the background. Hazel was not surprised to find them at the nearest seats to the boarding exit, clearly experienced travellers. Immediately, Mrs. Williams was all over Hazel like a rash.

"Do call us Gilbert and Susan, G & S to our friends, because we're heavily into all things dramatic and just love all the G & S operettas. You're not an afficionado I suppose?"

"Well yes, I do enjoy their work and I love the theatre…"

"Oh, good. Not that's there's much of that sort of thing in Madeira, a bit lacking in culture I'm afraid, but you can't have everything can you? I mean usually we go for the sun, don't we? Not this time of the year of course. I like a bit of a tan, but we girls have to be careful with our skin don't we? Don't want it to end up like a piece of leather. Plenty of moisturiser that's the secret and that's where our stage work helps, those grease paints are a really good source of hydration. Have you tried…?" At this point Gilbert interrupted,

"Susie darling, I don't think Mrs. Godwin…"

"Miss…" Hazel interjected.

"Sorry, Miss Godwin, wants to discuss cosmetics just now, she's trying to make contact with the others in our party."

Relieved that Susie had been stopped in her tracks, Hazel smiled at him. "Thanks Gilbert, just wanted to ask if you'd managed to speak to anyone else and to make sure you hadn't any problems."

Gilbert hesitated, "We did have a chat with the lady over there, Jane Roper, bit of a loner, I think."

Susie cut in, "Didn't seem to have much to say for herself. Couldn't quite make her out. Nice clothes though, expensive too." Then, at a sharp glance from Gilbert, Susie added, "Sorry, not my business…"

Brushing aside her apologies, Hazel excused herself and made her way over to Jane Roper. She realised at once what the Williams had been trying to say. Jane seemed rather ill at ease, as if afraid of saying the wrong thing. Seated next to her was the young couple Hazel knew had won this holiday in Madeira, in a competition staged by Primetime, her own travel company. The young woman was six or seven months pregnant and Hazel quickly learned this was their first time abroad. Introducing them to Jane, Hazel was surprised to note that in their company Jane suddenly relaxed and responded, if not enthusiastically, with at least some show of interest. The girl Sally's excitement about the holiday was very obvious. The husband, Tom, seemed somewhat withdrawn but Hazel warmed to them. They'd need a bit of looking after though, she'd make a note of that.

Jack Simmonds was next, tall, well-built and well-mannered! She made a mental note of the fact that he leapt to his feet as soon as she turned in his direction. The second thing of note was his accent. "Jack, surely you're from Australia? I mean… your accent?"

He grinned, "Well, ma'am, it's a long story and I

won't bore you with it now. I wasn't born there, but my grandmother was and my grandfather spent most of his life there. I'm afraid I'm stuck with the accent."

"Don't lose it, I think it's attractive. You're obviously well travelled so won't need much advice from me. Enjoy…!" With that Hazel moved down the line to the Landaus, Johann and Rachel, both Jewish sounding names, *Hope to goodness we haven't any anti-Semitic travellers on board!* Rachel, thirtyish, had the palest of skins, emphasising her dark eyes which were quite beautiful. They both worked in London and Johann said they were looking forward to a week's respite in Madeira before returning to the daily routine of coping with traffic, early starts and late returns home. The woman, Rachel, seemed rather aloof. Having dropped a rather large hint that the young pregnant girl and her husband hadn't been abroad before and were nervous, Hazel left them. Fingers crossed that they would keep an eye on Sally and Tom.

Eight down and five to go! Madge Miller, 40ish, dark curly hair, small and sparrow-like, was absorbed in a best seller but quickly moved her bag and smiled Hazel a welcome. "Hello Madge, have you been to Madeira before?"

"No, but it's always been on my wish list which never seems to get any shorter. I've loved what I've seen of it in travel books – stunning views, the connection with Churchill, and the world-famous Reid's Hotel – I really must go and have a look at that." Hazel smiled back. *What a surprise she's going to have – what a lovely, lovely surprise!*

David Griffin next, in his 50's she guessed, he seemed very much at ease, chatting to young Colin Seymour. Hazel quickly introduced herself and learned that David had been to Madeira before, but not at this time of the year. As she had guessed, Colin was an office worker, something to do with accounting. Although, he explained, he'd read Climate Change at university and having heard that Gran Canaria had invested heavily in wind turbines and Madeira was planning to do the same, he hoped during the holiday to find time to learn just how successful the energy saving had proved. David was a vet, owned his own company and was at a stage when he could hand over the reins to others when he felt like it.

Lucky him! Wish I could say the same. Goodness! perhaps he's the one, the secret's all about,...saying he's able to hand over the business at will, could just be a cover. I like him! And, no, it's not just because he might be sitting on a pile of money, although that would of course enhance the situation. He's comfortably large, has a disarming smile and eyes that twinkle. Good to have around.

Just time to greet Alexandre and Marie Moreau. Again, beautiful manners, but they don't seem to be making any effort to gel with the others as yet. If I remember from his paperwork, he's a medical man, I don't think she quoted any work. Hope they're not going to prove snooty!

At last they were boarding and with everyone seated and cabin baggage stowed, Hazel sank thankfully into her seat and closed her eyes, mulling over the events of the last 24 hours. How ready she had been to blow her top, if the unopened package was to say she'd been re-routed. Then she had read the enclosed letter.

Hazel,

This is to inform you that one of the tourists in your tomorrow's group has recently had a massive win in the European Lottery. The person in question, who wishes to remain anonymous, has requested that you and your entire group be transferred to Reid's for the period of their holiday, at the donor's expense. The excuse to be proffered, by the hotel, and you, is that the booked Orquidea hotel, one of Reid's smaller sister units, has had some unexpected construction problems and it has been necessary to make the transfer. Each envelope contains a cheque refunding all holiday costs already paid.

As it is traditional for diners at Reid's to wear evening dress, your group members are informed in their individual letters that suitable dresses, suits and necessary accessories will be at their disposal for the period of their stay. Information that all their holiday expenses will be covered, is also included.

With regard to the couple who won a holiday from our Company, their letter explains that a further holiday will be offered them at a date of their choosing.

The tourists are not to be told of the background circumstances unless the donor decides to reveal him or herself. The party are to remain under the assumption that these 'extras' are being provided as part of a random selection, in order to advertise and promote our Primetime Company.

Your own expenses are also covered and it has been stressed that should you want to upgrade any of the holiday excursions already planned this will not present a problem. Lucky you, Hazel. Enjoy!!

Whoever the winner was, he/she had certainly come up trumps and tomorrow should put some smiles on at least 13 faces. How nice for me to have something different from the same old routine. And what a challenge to determine our benefactor.

**

The arrival at Funchal passed smoothly, luggage collected and taken to the small coach waiting, numbers tallied, and they were ready for the off. A brief, quiet conversation with the driver with regard to the change of venue and Hazel grasped the microphone and stood up to face the group.

"Welcome to Madeira and I want to introduce to you Joao, our driver, who will be with us for the remainder of the week." A spatter of 'Hellos' and applause and she continued,

"Before we leave I am going to hand out some envelopes, one to each single traveller and one to each couple. Please do not open the envelope until I have finished the distribution as I want you all to read them together and whilst the coach is stationary."

Quickly she did the distribution and then, laughing, said, "On your marks, get set, go!" For a few moments after the sounds of paper being torn there was silence, then, "Wow!" this from Susie Williams, followed by exclamations all round, laughter, couples embracing and excited chatter. Sally and Tom, for whom Hazel had requested seats at the front of the coach looked stunned. Having won one holiday, they were now being told that a second one was on the cards. Sally, surreptitiously had a little weep – it was all too much.

Hazel decided it was time to pass on more information.

"When we arrive at Reid's we will be met by the Manager, the Housekeeper, the Maitre d' Hotel and the senior receptionist. This is unusual, but they are treating our visit as a special occasion. You will be given the keys to your rooms, which all face the sea." (Gasps of delight). Your luggage will be taken straight to your rooms, but as it is already one thirty we are asked to go straight to the Garden Room where a light buffet and coffee, or something stronger if you wish, are waiting.

"The dining room is a strict, full evening dress area." (Gasps of horror) "However, don't panic, as your letter stated, Reid's have arranged that for the duration of our stay, dresses and suits will be made available for you in these unexpected circumstances. After lunch, when back in your rooms and ready, please phone the Housekeeper who will send someone to escort you to the Wardrobe rooms so that you may select apparel for this evening and others if you so wish. Any minor adjustments will be taken care of by the staff.

"To allow time for all this I suggest we meet in the bar at 7.45 p.m. with dinner at 8.15p.m. Tonight there will be 3 tables for our use, two seating 4 and one 6. Tomorrow we will vary the seating. Breakfast will be in the Garden room and times are listed in your rooms, please sit wherever you wish. Each day I will post a list of the day's activities in the foyer. These are optional of course, but do let me know if you will *not* be participating, it helps when I'm doing a head count.

"This change of plan is exciting for all of us – a world famous five star hotel and nothing to pay, incredible! I know Christmas has just gone, but I think you'll agree from today's news it seems as if Santa's still with us." And, turning to the driver "Right Jo, I think that's all, let's go and give our new base the once over!"

**

How different they all looked in their full fig! Hazel felt rather glamorous herself, in lemon-yellow velvet, chosen because the colour accentuated her hazel eyes. Assembled in the bar the ladies provided a swathe-like rainbow of silks and satins whilst the men were transformed in their immaculate dinner jackets and bow ties. David and Jack, she decided, looked particularly attractive. Sally's 'bump' had been skilfully concealed and if husband Tom was feeling ill at ease he was managing to hide it very well and seemed to be chatting to Madge quite readily. *What a joy, I don't wonder they all seem happy, Hazel thought. Flowers and champagne in every room. Exquisite Christmas decorations everywhere, I could soon get accustomed to this sort of life-style!*

Being escorted to their table by the Maitre d'.was, for all of them, a moment to savour and by the time they were seated, the elegance of their surroundings, the exquisite napery and gleaming cutlery had reduced them to silence – almost! Susan Williams determined not to appear too over-awed started to chat to David Griffin and soon others had broken the ice and were talking to those seated next to them.

Good... Hazel thought. Several were now speaking to their fellow travellers for the first time. If we're to spend a week in each other's company, we must all be at ease with everyone else in our group. Tomorrow I'll tell them, apart from Sally and Tom, no hogging seats in the coach. They'll be expected to be in a different seat each day so that no-one can complain someone else always has the best views! It also means they're behind, in front of, or opposite a different set of people – all good for bonding!

Mmm...this dessert is scrumptious, Farofias the menu says, meringues cooked in lemon and something else and there's a flavour of cinnamon...dread to think how many calories I'll pile on this week. Time to turn the other way and chat to Jack.

That night as the lights dimmed in the Reid's bedrooms, the travellers, all tired after the events of the day, were soon asleep, with one exception, the person who had made it all possible. Staring at the ceiling, the donor smiled. It had worked, no longer a lonesome tourist. Already contact with others had been made and enjoyed. The money had certainly brought happiness to people here if their reactions were anything to go by, and certainly to *me* – it's a start! Smiling again, the donor turned over and switched off the light.

**

They awoke to a bright but cool morning and after breakfast, Hazel found them all assembled and ready to board the coach. She had explained that many of the flowers for which Madeira was famous might not be available at this time of the year, but the flower market and the fish market were both still wonderful to see and those would be their first points of call. The flower market exceeded her and their expectations. In Madeira's temperate climate it seemed that delicate flowers were rarely threatened by sharp frosts. The colours everywhere were startlingly brilliant. An unexpected and welcome surprise, especially for those with cameras, was the arrival, carried by four men, of an enormous tuna fish. Hazel explained,

"Because these fish live very far down in the ocean, to bring them straight up to the surface could result in them exploding – the same principle which applies to deep sea divers who, if brought up too quickly, experience what is known as 'the bends', which if not treated immediately and treated properly could prove fatal. So, fishing for tuna is handled very carefully."

Driver Jo drove them round Funchal so that they might get their bearings for future visits on foot, it was obvious to them all that it would be impossible to avoid fairly steep hills. Next they travelled on the coast road to Camara de Lobos, stopping for coffee and an opportunity to take photos of the splendid views.

"Tomorrow we'll go much further afield," Hazel told them. "right up into the mountainous region. I'm hoping you all had a good night's sleep, but yesterday was a tiring day, so I'm making today less so. We'll go back to the hotel for lunch and then you're on your own until dinner time, 7.0 for 7.30 tonight. Do explore the whole of the hotel and its beautiful gardens right on the edge of the sea. There are three pools and some of you might like a swim… one of the pools is heated! Again costumes can be provided, just ask. There are sun traps in the garden and sun rooms, so if you just want to sit and read, or admire the view, you'll have plenty of areas to choose from.

"We'll leave at 10.0 a.m. tomorrow and, as it will be cold at the higher altitude please make sure you have some very warm extra layers with you and sensible shoes for those who want to get out of the coach. And one other thing, if you suffer from vertigo, please do not take a window seat, there are steep roads for the coach to manoeuvre. Tomorrow we'll discuss arrangements for the firework display on Saturday night. You can either watch from the hotel gardens where there will be adequate provision in the way of seating, car rugs etc. and hot toddies to keep you warm, or, if you prefer it, Driver Jo will take you to a very good viewing point on the coast road and assures me that there will be flasks of hot coffee and Madeira wine to keep out any chill. Any questions? No, OK, then it's back to base please, Jo."

Interesting to see that David and Madge are sitting together and Jane is with Colin, I would have expected the two ladies to join up. It leaves Jack out on a limb though, I'd better look out for that tomorrow, if those 2 pairs occur again, I'll ask him to join me.

***

20

Chapter 2

The next morning saw them all assembled with, as Hazel had suggested, warmer clothes, sensible shoes and holdalls containing extra sweaters. No time was wasted in boarding and very soon they had left the town behind and were able to appreciate the stunning views of sea and countryside, from their very elevated position.

It had been, as Hazel had promised, a steep climb. They were all intrigued to learn that although they saw little or no livestock, there was on the island a considerable cattle population. She asked them to note the promontories jutting out from the cliffs and they saw that the majority each contained a single house with what appeared to be a small barn.

"That is where the cattle are kept," she explained. "At such heights and on a limited surface area it would be far too dangerous for animals to roam at will, so the occupants of the houses keep their cows in the small constructions you see, called palheiros."

"Not always, surely?" this from David, his concerns as a vet., surfacing.

"No, they are regularly exercised, but you will never see cattle grazing unattended."

"But isn't that rather cruel?" someone asked.

"By our standards, yes, I suppose. But I think you'll agree that different people down the years have determined their own cultures and if they appear to be working satisfactorily, then we are not in a position to be too critical."

"Do people live in those houses all the time?" Madge wanted to know.

"It varies. Some stay for months at a time, others for shorter periods. Years ago there were splendid houses built on the sides of the mountains by rich people, who went there to avoid the heat of the summer."

"But," Madge hesitated, "how do people get up there to those small houses we can see now? And with a cow? It seems impossible!"

"I agree, but when settlers were in the process of clearing the forests for agriculture they realised they would need irrigation for their crops, so they made a system of channels and tunnels, levadas, carrying water, from high in the mountains down to the fields and villages below. I think the farmers who live here today will have made use of both new road structures and the channels and tunnels made years ago.

"But let's press on, I'm sure like me, you're all ready for a cup of coffee."

Soon they were at a rather tired looking wooden building, but attitudes quickly changed when Hazel informed them Churchill had been a frequent visitor. A smiling buxom lady gave instructions to her young assistant and coffee and hot chocolate appeared almost immediately. The lady in charge then produced what she insisted were home-made biscuits, so beautifully packaged that the ladies in the group raised eyebrows and smiled at each other, recognising the professional touch. Having tasted the samples provided, the ladies nodded their approval and the owner was delighted with the number of packs purchased. As Hazel said, "They will make nice little gifts and far better than some of the knick knacks on offer. Now, onward and upward."

There were squeals from both Sally and Susan at the next hairpin bend and after a further few miles they were aware, even inside the coach, that the temperature had dropped sharply. Once they were on a clear stretch of road running parallel with the edge of the ravine there was a more relaxed atmosphere. The French couple and Johann and Rachel all appeared to be asleep and Sally's head was on Tom's shoulder.

"What was that?" Madge Miller sat up sharply. "A sonic boom – I've heard it before in Switzerland. Oh Lord, it usually means …."

Before she could say any more a shudder passed through the coach, followed by cracking sounds and then they felt the coach falling slowly, but surely, downwards. There were screams and cries and then silence, as suddenly the momentum came with a shudder and a grating noise to a grinding stop.

Hazel tried to bring herself back to reality. *What could have happened? If they'd gone over the edge why hadn't they crashed to the bottom of the ravine?*

At her side, Jack Simmonds took her hand "Are you OK?"

"I think so…but we've come to a halt, surely…?"

"We're wedged on something which must be supporting us. It seems to be darker on our side of the coach, as if we could be close to the cliff face." He half turned his head and called, "Is anyone injured?"

Feeble cries of "No" and "I don't think so."

"Listen, all of you", Jack said, "I know it's scary, but *please,* do not move, for whatever reason, unless you're told to do so. It is very important. Those on the left side of the coach do *not* look out of the window. Do you understand?"

Feeble responses of 'Yes' and Jack started to get to his feet. Leaning forward he touched driver Jo on the shoulder. There was no reaction and Jack could see a lot of blood on Jo's right arm but felt a pulse in his neck. The coach door had been split on its fold down the middle and Jack eased first one segment out to give himself enough room to get through and then finding himself on the steps of the coach with solid ground about two feet beneath him, he eased out the second section. From outside he could see what he had half expected had happened, the coach had slid down the ravine side, at first balanced on a section of the roadway. As this had crumbled and fallen away the forward section of the coach had, to its occupants' good fortune, landed on top of one of the small houses they had seen on their drive. It was now stationary at an angle with the right hand side close to the ravine wall and the left side more elevated. His vision blocked by the rest of the house, he guessed they could not afford to take any chances. They might, on the other side of the coach, or at the rear, be very close to the edge of the promontory.

Jack stepped back onto the coach steps. "Listen folks, as I call your name I want you to slowly cross over to the other side of the coach, this side. Don't worry if someone is sitting in that seat, this is no time to be prissy – sit on their knees, if necessary. It's important we get as much weight as possible over here. Tom, help Sally over into my seat.

"Good. Now Marie move onto your husband's knee and Madge slowly move across into the space she has left beside him.

"Susan do the same, sit on Gilbert's knee so that Rachel can move across into the space by you and as soon as they are settled, Johann move across to the seat behind them.

"Good. Now David, keeping as much of your weight as possible on this side of the coach, please come and join me here."

Thank God it's daylight, how would we have managed otherwise.

"You next," Jack said, holding out his arms to Hazel.

"No, take Sally."

"I want you out here first, to help Sally. I'm going to need Tom before he joins you."

How quickly he's assessed the situation and taken control, Hazel thought.

"David, as each one reaches you, please urge them to go as quickly as they can forward, until they come to the end of the house. The door is probably round that corner. I want to get everyone away from this edge in case more rocks come down."

And so it went on, holding their breaths with each movement as steadily, one by one, they were removed from the coach until only the driver was left wedged in his seat. He was alive but obviously injured and, unexpectedly, it was Tom who seemed to know how the seat itself could be more easily removed with Jo still in it and without running the risk of aggravating the injuries and flow of blood.

To David's amazement as he approached the end of the house with the other travellers following, he saw ahead, a light... someone holding a lantern. It was a small, very old man peering down the side of the house. David called out "Hello, can you help us? We're English." The man didn't respond but holding the lantern higher he motioned them forward, urging them round the corner until they saw the door. He flung it open and the men quickly ushered the ladies inside. Hazel helped Sally to a seat and, seeing that Madge appeared on the point of fainting, signalled to David, Madge too, was then quickly seated. They looked around and saw they were in a kitchen cum store room with a curtain which covered just half of its far end. The old man drew that back to reveal another small area with a table, an ancient settee and 3 chairs and, most welcome of all, a wood burning stove alight and giving off some heat. It appeared to be a single unit with a small black oven alongside it.

It's the smallest oven I've ever seen, but, Hallelulia, thank goodness for some heat.

All is not lost! All the ladies were now ushered into that room thankful to sit and be under cover and out of what was now extremely cold air. All were ashen faced and seemed to be braced for further problems.

Hazel looked around her in horror. Never had she experienced anything like this.

My whole group traumatised and stuck somewhere on the side of a cliff – God knows where. Supposing, Heaven forbid, there should be another landslip and more of the face of the ravine come down. What then? At least most of the group seemed to have suffered only grazes and whiplash from the impact of hitting the house roof, which was a miracle, but their white faces revealed shock and inward terror at what they had just endured and what might lie ahead.

David was talking to the other men and clearly saying they must now go back and see if Jack and Tom had been able to get the driver from his seat. A mist had come down from the mountains and visibility was fading. At this point, the old man, still silent, came from the kitchen and lit several more lanterns, passing them over to David, Colin, Johann and Alexandre. Gilbert appeared to have hurt his hand and Susan was trying to clean it with a handkerchief. Seeing this the old man disappeared for a moment returning with pieces of clean white rag and motioning her to the small pump in one corner of the kitchen.

Sally seemed to have handled the situation well, but said she was very thirsty. Hazel made motions of drinking to the old man and he nodded and emerged again from the kitchen, this time with a tray on which was a bottle, some plastic cups and a large jug of milk.

"My goodness," this from Susan, "Madeira wine, as I live and breathe. Just the ticket to make us all feel better." With this she shook the old man's hand warmly and smiled her thanks.

She was right of course. And bless her, she's removed some of the tension whilst I'm forgetting my responsibilities. Must get on the phone and let people know where we are.

With that Hazel took her mobile phone from her jacket pocket and phoned Reid's, asking them to alert the police and other services, giving them a very rough outline of their position. It was now dusk and the odds of anything being done tonight had disappeared. She was in charge and must organise some sort of arrangements for her group.

As if reading her mind, the old man came to her, his hand extended and taking her outside by the light of his lantern showed her the palheiro where his two cows were kept and to one side of it a small shed housing a chemical toilet.

Praise the Lord, it's something I'd been dreading, my ladies having to squat down somewhere in the middle of nowhere. This really is a bonus. I must go and convey the good news - after what we've experienced they're probably all desperate by now.

But before this could be done sounds from the side of the house indicated that the men were returning and first of all came Johann and Alex holding their lanterns aloft so that Jack and Tom carrying the driver still in his seat could see the passage way. The seat safely placed in a corner of the kitchen, Marie, her colour returned was, surprisingly, the first to come forward and examine Jo.

"I suspect he has an abdominal injury from the impact of the wheel when the coach finally struck the corner of the house and he blacked out with the pain and shock. His arm is broken, but we can deal with that. I think that he should have a small amount of the wine, it can do him no harm and might help him to regain consciousness. Then we must somehow remove him from this chair and see that he lies flat so that his internal organs have the opportunity to readjust."

Thank goodness, she seems to know what she's talking about and here's David. I know he's a vet, but we're all animals after all and must have quite similar reactions.

David agreed with Marie and Alex was also nodding his head, so together they endeavoured to get a small amount of wine down Jo's throat. Within seconds some colour had filtered back into his face and opening his eyes he looked around him, clearly puzzled.

"It's OK Jo, you're safe now." David's manner was reassuring. *We hope. Just don't let there be another landslip or any other rocks descending on us.*

The old man had approached to see the driver and suddenly spoke to him in Portuguese. When Jo responded with a few words, Hazel sent up another fervent prayer of thanks. *Now, at last they could communicate with the old man through the driver and ask questions, assuming Jo remained able to respond of course.*

David was attempting to ask if there was a bed where the driver could be laid and it was not until Jo was able to repeat the word in Portuguese that the old man understood.

He led the way to the end of the room where the ladies were seated and drew back the curtain. There was a bed, a large bed, but the far side of it was covered with debris from the roof. Hazel was heartened though, to see that the bed had two mattresses, was covered with a blanket and thick patchwork quilt and that an open ottoman contained several blankets. They could at least make 2 beds out of this one; then, as if reading her thoughts the old man left them, returning with a flat palette of straw and motioning that he had many more. Of course, they could create their own beds with

28

palettes and blankets. They would manage. But what about food?

Never had Hazel been so thankful to see the bags which David and Colin had retrieved, oh so carefully, from the coach. If they had no other food tonight at least there were quite a number of packets of biscuits here. And, knowing her compatriots, it was quite likely that some of these bags contained bars of chocolate carried by so many ladies, on both long and short journeys to stave off pangs of hunger. How often she'd heard them saying 'Well you never know if you're going to be held up in a traffic jam, or an accident hold-up.'

The call from the police seemed to reverberate in the little house. It was as she had expected. Nothing could be done until daylight when the situation would be assessed.

Should there be anything for which they had a desperate need she was to let them know – insulin requirements, painkillers, etc., then these could be dropped by helicopter at dawn. Did they need food or blankets, these could also be arranged... tonight they were on their own.

The priority now was to get the driver out of the chair and as comfortable as possible. Together the men set about removing the debris from the bedroom area. The old man produced a plastic trough and this was soon filled with rubbish from the bed's edge. At Hazel's suggestion, in view of the danger of further falling rocks, the bed was moved forward, so that it projected into the seating area. The ottoman was also pulled out – it would provide another couple of seats. Then, once the floor appeared tolerably clean, one mattress was lifted on to it, providing two places on which to lie down. There were already sheets on the bed, which Marie removed, a linen tablecloth was found to take the place of a sheet and they were ready for their invalid.

Tom's unexpected familiarity with the chair's construction and the location in the dashboard glove cupboard of a screw driver, meant that the men were able to dismantle it whilst still occupied. Colin and Jack found a wooden window shutter and this was held under Jo whilst, piece by piece, they removed the chair's sections. He was carried to the bed on the board and, at Marie's suggestion, transferred to the mattress still lying on it. He had cried out with pain when being moved, but now seemed more aware of what was happening around him. Marie's request for a support so that she and Alex might make Jo's arm more comfortable was quickly found. Susan produced a folding walking stick and suggested it was broken into pieces as required, whilst Rachel and Sally produced scarves which could be used both for wrapping the supports and creating a sling. And when Jane asked if the paracetomol tablets in her bag were of any use, Marie was quick to seize them, saying they would help.

The old man signalled to Colin and Johann and they followed him outside and into the palheiro. There they were surprised to find a clean and well ordered byre much larger than they'd expected. The two cows were lying in a pen and behind them at the far end was a low doorway obviously sited for brushing manure and soiled straw outside. At one side of the barn was a whole rack of straw palettes, both narrow and wide, in front of which stood a number of milking buckets and a stool, the other side was stacked with bags of animal feed whilst in the middle of the room was a clean formica topped table with a variety of jugs and bottles and underneath it a container with clean cloths, scrubbing brushes, a box full of rags and even a bottle of disinfectant. They were impressed!

The old man pointed to the palettes and was obviously suggesting they take more into the house. A pile was taken in and propped against the kitchen wall, until needed.

On their return they found Susan and Jane, at Hazel's request, had put on the small well-scrubbed table whatever edibles people had with them. It was a motley assortment. Biscuits, packets of mints and pastilles, 4 precious bars of chocolate, 3 apples and an orange.

The old man following Joshua and Johann in with the palettes, seeing the assortment of foods laid out, at first appeared startled, his brow furrowed, then he grinned at the assembled company, the brown leather-like skin creasing in all directions. Moving towards a cupboard in the kitchen, with a flourish he opened the door and produced a giant-sized ham and a loaf of black bread. Placing them in the middle of the sweets he grinned again showing an array of gum and blackened teeth and lifting his eyebrows as if to say "I knew I could surprise you."

There was a gale of laughter and a ripple of applause, so much so that Jo called from his bed, in English, "What is happening?" David explained about the ham and motioned to the old man to come to the bedside and talk to Jo, hoping that hearing his own language would prove a boost to his recovery.

Now there was frenzied activity. Alex and Johann were put in charge of carving the ham and Rachel and Madge in carefully sharing out the loaf. Susan rummaged in the kitchen and found an assorted collection of items which might be useful, a few pieces of cutlery and... another bottle of Madeira wine. Showing it to the old man and clearly asking the question as to whether they could use it, she received another gummy grin and went ahead ensuring everyone had a drink.

The small oven at the side of the wood stove had virtually gone unnoticed but they now realised this was a total unit and it could be used for cooking or for keeping things warm. Seeing Hazel examining it closely, the old man took her arm and led her into the kitchen, pointing out a small brazier and a very large, well-worn kettle. Putting a match to the brazier filled with wood chippings, he filled the kettle at the pump and after a few moments whilst he waited for the fire to get established, placed the kettle on top of it, grinning at her obvious delight.

The question of keeping themselves warm was something which had started to worry Hazel. They were in a mountainous region, it was already quite dark and feeling colder by the minute. Now with another item giving off heat, things didn't look quite so bleak. The number in the party meant that they would produce a good volume of body heat, but the temperature was likely to drop much further in the next few hours and cold air was coming through the gaps in the bedroom roof. She decided that, where room, the palettes would have to be laid alongside each other to ensure combined body-heat. It was asking a lot from comparative strangers but she couldn't see any alternative – although she did wonder how the old man had managed.

Again it was as if he had read her thoughts. Now he was foraging at the no-man's land at the far end of the bedroom and she saw he had uncovered another ottoman. He motioned her forward and trying not to look up at the jagged edges of the roof structure and the clearly visible underside of the coach front, Hazel moved towards him. Once more she saw his toothy gummy grin as he held out thick trousers and jackets, all obviously hand-made, pieces of tapestry layered with embroidery, several more thick blankets and at the bottom a number of packages carefully wrapped in tissue paper. It truly was a treasure chest.

Just as Hazel started planning their sleeping arrangements, her mobile rang. The police wanted an update on their situation and requirements for the next day, adding that unfortunately the following morning's forecast was not good, with mountain mist lingering until mid afternoon, when hopefully it would have been burnt off by the sun. Marie's requirements for Jo were painkillers, grip-type bandages which would support his arm, yoghurts or any soft food which would not impact on any abdominal injuries he had and antiseptic for surface cuts and bruises.

Hazel asked for more blankets, loo rolls, cartons of soup, cereals as they had plenty of milk; bread, cheese, rice, bars of chocolate and some energising drinks would all be welcome. Adding, "A few bars of soap, towels and facecloths would not come amiss." Then, embarrassed, "Some ladies and men's underpants would help and ladies' special towels, if you get my drift. We have a lady here who is about seven months pregnant, please ask a doctor if there is anything we should have to help her through this ordeal." The helicopter, she was informed, would be overhead at 7.30 a.m., but it was stressed that should the weather deteriorate, the drop would have to be delayed.

"What about the tunnels?" Hazel asked, "would it not be possible to take the driver down to the valley that way? And couldn't our other needs be brought up via one of the levadas?"

"Sorry ma'am," came the reply. "In other circumstances it would have been possible. Unfortunately, we know that some of the bigger tunnels are blocked with fallen rocks, we haven't been able to check them all as yet. Our scientists tell us we cannot chance any of the levadas or narrow tunnels for two to three days until the land has had chance to settle. They also advise that you keep as far away from the ravine wall as possible. The helicopter is definitely our best way of providing you with assistance and it may well have to be your eventual escape route."

With that dismal prognosis, Hazel had to be satisfied. *Better not scare them all to death, with that info. Quite a lot of moderation required there I think, but must discuss it with someone first. One of the men? David, or Jack? Both, on second thoughts and Jane, so as to balance the sexes. They all seem level-headed and the men definitely were able to cope with crises as required. One question, Mr. Policeman, just how can we keep away from the cliff wall when the loo is almost touching it?*

"Well, what did they say?" Susan, hands on hips was watching Hazel closely, and with a certain amount of suspicion.

"Oh, they're happy to drop everything we need – at dawn, weather permitting. So, as soon as we've had something to eat, we'll get the bedding, such as it is, sorted. Then anyone who wants to lie down and try and sleep can do so, we're going to be awake early in the morning."

There were murmurs of agreement then they all looked the other way when a bucket and bottle were discreetly carried through to Driver Jo's quarters. In an effort at distraction, Hazel exclaimed, "You people in charge of food have done a wonderful job – I particularly love the napery." This, as she pointed to the 15 individual tissues, on each of which was laid three slices of ham, a chunk of bread, 2 squares of chocolate and a slice of apple.

"Yes, Rachel came up with that idea," Madge said "she had one pack and Marie had another."

"Brilliant! – David, Jane and Jack and I are going into the kitchen for a few minutes, so I'll let you know when the kettle boils. What about cups?" Hazel suddenly realised that there were probably no more than four in the house.

"Actually, we struck oil there – found a pack of cardboard beakers at the bottom of the kitchen cupboard, but I think we'll have to ask people to wash their own out when they've finished, or there won't be enough to go round." If Madge thought this would be met with disapproval she was wrong.

"Well done, you carvers and meal preparers have done a good job. We're going to drop the kitchen curtain for a while to form some sort of plan for the morning's events."

Jane and the two men felt Hazel had been quite right in not divulging the depressing news given to her by the police. Jane's comment was "We all have enough to cope with, so there's no use in piling on the agony, better to face each new difficulty as it arises."

"I've just had an awful thought," this from Hazel. "Am I right in thinking that Jews can't eat pork? Where will that leave Johann and Rachel?"

David was reassuring, "I think you'll find that in unexpected and extreme circumstances, which this certainly is, their religion gives them absolution if they have no other choice of food. I'll have a quiet word with them if you like. I'll get back to you if there's a problem, Hazel."

It was decided that once the kettle boiled and tea was made all the women, except Hazel, should go into the kitchen and have their drinks, whilst the men set out the palettes. It was agreed that Jack and Colin should share on the ravine side of the bedroom, next to Driver Jo's bed, available to assist him if necessary, with Sally and Tom together on the mattress on the other side of the bed. Hazel's comment, "Sally is, more than any of us, likely to feel discomfort if we ask her to lie on one of the palettes," was met with approval.

The three married couples, Landaus, Williams and Moreaus would each share the wider palettes, Jane and Madge would share and David and Hazel would have the narrow ones, wherever there was a space. Before they retired David asked Jack if, when they had earlier found the window shutter there had been any others.

"Yes, quite a pile of them, obviously used when it gets too hot and when it's very cold – guess the old man hadn't got round to putting them up. Why?"

"Give me a hand to bring some in will you? I've got an idea. And Colin, I suppose you haven't seen any rope or cord lying around anywhere?" The three men were soon busily occupied and then invited the women to come in and see their handiwork. A screen had been erected round the pump and alongside it was a small table from the sitting room complete with a bowl and some clean cloths.

"There ladies, all ready for the morning! You have to fill the kettle and then put it on the brazier and you'll have warm water to wash in privacy." David was proud of their handiwork.

"Just a minute Dave," Colin dashed off through to the bedroom coming back with a piece of embroidered tapestry from the ottoman. Carefully he arranged it over the wooden shutter, "Just so no-one can peep in through the holes." They laughed and then the ladies exclaimed at the quality of the needlework.

"It's much too good to be used like this, it's quite beautiful." They were all in agreement, but it had been a long nerve-wracking day and they were weary. Returning to their allotted palettes there was no question of stripping off in this public arena. Shoes were removed and outer jackets, but although the stove was well stacked with logs the thought of the spiky straw scratching bare legs convinced them that they must stay as covered as possible.

Another plus, Hazel thought. I hadn't realised that all the women, even Sally, were wearing trousers – that's a blessing, however small, for all of us. Heavens, I've forgotten someone, where's the old man? He had his supper, now I can't see him.

"Dave, where's the old man?"

He grinned, "I had a feeling you'd suddenly realise someone was missing. He's in the palheiro."

"What? He can't say there all night."

"He's quite adamant that's what he's going to do. When I saw him going to the door, I guessed what he was up to and after a lot of shivering on my part to indicate that it would be much too cold, he grinned and from behind the door he took a thick jacket, a woollen hat and an old blanket. He signalled to me that he had done this many times before, when calves were being born. Actually he ought to be on the stage, his miming was excellent. Don't forget he's got the straw to keep him warm plus the things he took out there with him."

"Still, it's a bit much – this is his house after all, it's not right that we've turned him out."

"I don't think he sees it like that. Come on it's time we joined the others – I'm turning this lantern out. There are two in the other room, one at the front near the stove and one by the window at the back, there are candles next to them and matches in case either go out, and someone is desperate for some light. Jack and Colin have their own lantern and we've pulled out that old curtain which divided the room, Jack managed to reach some nails overhead, so it screened the bed and gave Driver Jo some privacy."

"Is he going to be OK, David?"

"Can't say until he's been X-rayed and we know the

damage, but get to bed, you look exhausted."

***

Chapter 3

Exhausted they may have been, but it was a difficult night, with sleep elusive, sometimes for hours at a time. They hadn't been aware how crackly the straw was until they attempted to turn over or move a few inches. Multiplying that by the number of people in the room meant that there seemed to be crackles from all directions.

And I thought I'd have to make sure they were up before the helicopter came, just in case there was a change of plan. Someone's up already and it's (peering at her watch) just five o'clock! Ugh. I suppose I'd better show some leadership and go and join whoever it is.

Hazel was not surprised to find Susan washed and, if not looking refreshed, at least not quite as exhausted as the previous night. Soon they were joined by the other ladies, anxious to freshen up, and once they were all in the kitchen, the men stowed the palettes and blankets back in the kitchen leaving the room clear.

Accompanying Marie to see what state Driver Jo was in they were pleased to see that he had regained more colour, his arm was comfortable but told them his abdomen was still very painful and tender. Quietly Marie said to Hazel, "I will be glad when the helicopter comes. I'm going to give him some more paracetomol now, but then we're down to the last four tablets."

For the first time the members of the group decided to venture outside to see in daylight what had happened last night. It was not what they wanted to see. Visibility was down to approximately two metres and David and Jack were very insistent that until that improved, they were safer inside.

At 6.50 a.m. Hazel's phone rang and back inside the room the tension was tangible. It was as they feared,

"Miss Godwin, it's bad news I'm afraid. We've loaded the helicopter with all your requirements, but if you have looked out of the window, you'll be aware of the problem, it's just too dangerous for us to fly at the moment. We are told that by two or three o'clock things should improve, so I'm afraid...."

"There's one other thing. Now we know the location of the house you're in, we feel you should know something else. The owner is Manuel Ronaldo, who is 78. His wife, Madeleine, died up there 3 weeks ago and she was brought down via a levada to be buried in the churchyard in the valley. She was very well known in Funchal, famous on two counts. One, for her exquisite embroidery, which sold at a high price. And secondly, because people believed she had second sight and could see into the future. I wouldn't know about that, never having had occasion to ask her for help. Manuel has two daughters here in the valley, but he insisted on going back to his home to look after the cows and to sort out anything he wished to keep. He then intends selling the house and palheiro so that he can move to the valley and live with one of his girls and her family."

"Thank you for that. We haven't been able to establish his name, so that will be a help, also knowing what's happened, so recently. We'll look forward to seeing you as soon as possible."

"Yes, I'm so sorry."

Told the news, the group was quiet with a few quietly shed tears from Sally and Rachel. It was just 7.0 a.m. and there would now be 7 or 8 hours to fill, with little or no food and a choice of milk or tea to drink.

How are we going to fill the time? Even after yesterday some of them hardly know each other... Hazel my girl, get to grips with yourself, therein lies your answer. If they don't know each other yet, there couldn't be a better time to alter that than now.

Another decision made, Hazel started to put it into action.

"Sorry chaps, bring just a few more palettes back would you and blankets, enough to make another seat. If you could move the table over by Jo's curtain please, he should sleep now he's had some pills. I want everyone to have a seat and be as comfortable as we can make it.

"Good, thank you. Now, are you sitting comfortably?" A few titters from the group, "No, I'm not about to introduce Children's Hour.

"Someone once said we all have a book inside us – perhaps that's rather an exaggeration, but I do think we each have a story to tell, whether it be brief or lengthy. Some of us here come from, or have experiences of, different parts of the world. We're of varying ages so have lived through changing patterns of existence – sometimes from choice, sometimes because they were thrust upon us. It may be that stories told us by other, older members of our families have changed our outlooks on the world. Perhaps the messages they conveyed have made us, in turn, more sensitive and aware of certain situations.

"I wondered if we might pass some of the time, whilst waiting for our rescuers, by telling each other of some of those things we will always remember, whether sad or joyful. The stories might be your own, perhaps passed to you by members of your family, or an experience of someone you know. It doesn't matter whether they're long or short. Together we have shared something frightening and we must all be grateful that we are here and safe. In other circumstances although travelling together as a group, we might have stayed here in Madeira alone, or with our partners, separated from the rest of the party for the whole holiday. This event has made us depend on and help each other

41

where possible. Together we have become a unit which has known fear, joy in survival, and perhaps faith. We still have difficulties to face and together we can do it.

"Some of you will be familiar with Chaucer's tales of the Canterbury Pilgrims. Men and women from differing walks of life setting out on their journey to Canterbury Cathedral and finding that when they stopped at a tavern for the night, they could pass the time and entertain each other with their own stories. I think it's time we did something similar, telling each other anecdotes, or whole stories, whatever you wish. What do you think?"

There was some shuffling of feet and avoiding of eyes until finally, Tom stood up and said, "I think it sounds a pretty good idea and it if helps, I'll start us off."

"Thank you Tom, that would be great." *Who would have thought it? Bless him, just what's needed.*

"Should I remain standing?" he asked

"No, don't let's be formal. Just move so we can all see you and probably hear better."

Without more ado, he perched himself on the edge of the table and began...

"I wonder how many of you are familiar with the word 'scrumping'? My grandfather lived in Yorkshire and that word meant helping yourself to apples from gardens and orchards which didn't belong to you. At that time it was common practice amongst young lads and no-one took it very seriously.

"This is my grandfather's story really, but he passed it on to his son and my father to me, as a warning to young lads who might think they can get away – I won't say with murder, but if not careful, they might find themselves involved in one.

"When Granddad was about ten years old after school and at weekends he'd go out with his mates to

42

have, as they used to say 'a bit of a laugh'. One day, looking over a wall at the edge of a field they saw that the ground under the trees near the edge was littered with apples. There was no-one around, so within seconds the four of them were over the wall and cramming apples into their pockets and down the necks of their sweaters, as fast as they could.

"As usual the lads were laughing and chatting until suddenly they were stopped in their tracks by a roar from behind them. "What the 'ell do you think you're doing?"

"It was the farmer, legs astride, face as red as a beetroot and, most terrifying of all, holding a shotgun! The youngest lad, Tim, who was always a bit cheeky, said "Sorry Mister...we didn't think they was anybody's – a lot are rotten."

"The man, obviously very drunk, staggered towards him shouting "Don't you answer me back, you young varmint", raised the gun and shot him. As Tim slumped to the ground, the other boys screamed with shock and ran for the wall, scrabbling and diving to get over it and out of the man's way. Once over the other side they used the wall for cover and keeping low down, ran as fast as they could away from the nightmare they'd just witnessed. A quick glance behind them now and again and they saw the drunkard was not following. Ahead of them a man in his garden had heard the shot and was at the gate looking down the road. The boys raced towards him, shouting and trying to tell him what had happened. At first he couldn't decipher what they were saying through the tears pouring down their grubby faces. When he did understand he ran indoors to phone the police.

"His wife had heard the commotion and seeing the three boys with their tear-stained white faces, knew at once that if they'd been involved in a schoolboy prank it had gone seriously wrong. She shooed them into the kitchen and whilst her husband tried to send messages to their homes, sat them down, poured out glasses of ginger beer, telling them to drink slowly and take some deep breaths. All they could think of was the blood which had spouted from Tim's chest and the way his little body had crumpled. Soon they heard the sirens of a police car and ambulance. In three quarters of an hour they were all back at home being alternately cuddled for being alive and chastised for doing something so stupid.

"Tim had died instantly and the farmer was charged with manslaughter. His defence was that the boys were trespassing on his land and stealing his property, but the prosecution pointed out that down the years boys had always gone 'scrumping 'for apples, especially in what appeared to be a wild, uncared for piece of land. Crucially they added, the farmer had been very drunk, resulting in abnormal behaviour. The punishment he'd administered for a childish escapade had cost a young boy his life.

"The farmer was sent to prison for three years. For my grandfather and the other two boys involved it was the hardest lesson they ever learned and one they'd never forget."

Grinning at Sally, Tom added, "We don't know the sex of our baby, but if it's a boy, I can assure you, when he's older, one of the first things I'll be teaching him, is never take what isn't yours – it can have very dangerous consequences."

There was a ripple of applause and before Tom went back to his seat, a question from Madge, "What do you do for a living, Tom? The men probably know, but we women don't. We were all amazed that you managed to get Driver Jo's seat out of the coach and dismantle it so that he could lie down."

"My first job was as an apprentice at a firm which built coaches. I was with them for ten years, then decided to move on. I'd studied at night-time and taken a degree in engineering , that enabled me to find work as a trainee teacher at a Technical College and two years later as a fully fledged teacher. So, having learned how to put coaches together and their seating – I won't say what we did was easy because of the impact, but I was probably better equipped to tackle the job here than others."

"We congratulate you on that, Tom," Hazel said, "and on your story. It was sad but I did say happy or sad and it may well be that it's the latter which leaves the greater mark on our lives and memories. Now, who's next?"

To everyone's amazement Tom now assisted Sally to her feet. Grinning at Hazel he said, "She insisted, Hazel, and rather than upset her in her delicate condition, I thought it best to let her go ahead." With that he placed a chair in the middle of the floor, walking Sally over to it and seating her there.

"I keep telling Tom, I'm pregnant, not an invalid. I just remembered a very interesting little anecdote which occurred when I was teaching. It was a large school with about 500 children aged 9-14. Because of the large numbers and because so many stayed to school for dinner there were always two sittings. In my class were twins, a girl, Ella, quite tall and very overweight and a boy small and thin. Alarmed at the girl's weight, the school nurse referred Ella to a doctor and she was put on a strict diet. After a few weeks it was obvious that she had lost no weight and the doctor was baffled. One day I was on second dinner duty and as I crossed the foyer into the dining hall I saw Ella in the group leaving the hall on the other side. A typical extrovert she waved and called out to me 'It's a lovely dinner today, Miss', then disappeared in a sea of children.

"Once inside the dining hall I stood until all the children were settled in their places, then asked them to stand for grace. As I waited for complete silence I looked across the hall and there on the far side was Ella. Now I knew why she wasn't losing weight! As far as Ella was concerned two sittings for dinner meant two dinners and that was what she had been having for the past few weeks. We were able to laugh about it in the staffroom and left it in the capable hands of the doctor to explain, again, what she must and mustn't do.

"I'm sorry my little story is about food, just at a time when we are all preferring not to even think about it. It's just that Tom's story was sad and I thought I'd like to add this to make you all smile." Tom was already on his feet and returned her to her seat as the others laughed and clapped.

Susan stood up, smiling rather shyly. Looking at her, Hazel decided this was a different Susan from the self-important, giggling woman of a few days ago. Now she appeared composed and confident, as if totally at ease. Moving her chair slightly to ensure she could see everyone's face and that they could see and hear her, Susan sat down again and began.

"I was first on a stage when I was 8 years old. My family were Methodists which meant for us children, twice to Sunday School on Sundays and as adults, twice to chapel. One very important day, if not *the* most important day in the church calendar was the annual Bazaar. The opener was chosen in a three year rotation from the Junior and Senior Sunday Schools and the adult chapel-goers. To say that my mother was thrilled when, just before my eighth birthday, I was elected as Opener from the Juniors would be a serious understatement. My parents had separated when I was 3 years old and Mam had had a hard time with 3 children – I have an older sister and brother – having to work whenever and wherever possible to keep us fed and clothed.

"Just how she managed to save enough money to buy the material for the dress I was to wear, I'll never know. It was turquoise taffeta and a kind neighbour turned it into the most gorgeous thing I had ever owned. With it was a small matching drawstring bag. In that long beautiful dress, I felt like a princess.

"I knew I had to make a speech in front of a lot of people. The church hall was large and the bazaar stalls were always set round the perimeter with seats in the centre area. I was told all the chairs would be full and that though there would be a microphone, I must speak up so that everyone could hear. I was given a story which I could tell in any way that I wished. This is it.

"Brother Benedict loved walking and one day he left the monastery where he lived and walked for many miles until he reached a beautiful lush-green valley, one he had never seen before. Benedict also loved plants and flowers and he suddenly noticed a plant which was new to him. Stooping down he examined it closely. The leaves were quite shiny, a bright green, and from the centre stems cascaded small bell-like flowers, the colour of pearls and almost translucent. Taking a few more paces he saw that there were many other identical plants, all thriving and healthy. Taking from his pocket the small garden fork which he always had with him, he gently prised two of the precious plants from their surroundings. Wrapping them carefully in his handkerchief he set off back to the monastery.

"The plants were lovingly planted in the garden there and nurtured during the coming months by Brother Benedict. Soon he found that they had grown and spread and within two short years there was a whole bank of the delicate flowers. Visitors to the monastery all exclaimed at their beauty and asked their name – the other monks smiled and said, "They came to us with no name, but we have christened them, to us they are Brother Benedict's Lilies of the Valley."

"I don't know how much truth there is in that story. What I do know is that it set me on a path of loving lilies of the valley and drama for life. As a teenager, once I had started working in an office and had enough money I took lessons and joined first of all a Youth Club drama group and later, an adult group.

"Sometimes dramatic moments in the theatre are produced quite unexpectedly. Once we were performing 'Murder in the Cathedral' – for those who aren't familiar with it, it's the story of how Henry II fell out with Thomas a Beckett and in a moment of fury because Beckett would not do what he was asked , the King stormed out of the room saying "Will no one rid me of this troublesome priest?" When some of the King's knights heard this, they decided to go ahead and do just that.

"I was a member of the chorus, choral speech that is, not singing, and the performance was in a large church with our choral group moving around to different parts of the church as the story unfolded. To achieve the right atmosphere the church was lit by candles. It was evening and a man walking down the road outside saw the flickering lights through the window and assuming the church must be on fire called the fire brigade. Just as the play got to the crucial moment when Thomas a Beckett reached the high altar and the knights moved forward, swords raised to kill him, the front door of the church burst open and the firemen stormed in.

"Of course we were able to laugh about it afterwards and made sure people were able to see the correct version another evening, but we all remembered the shock of seeing those yellow helmets and jackets bursting in on us. I don't know who amongst us were the most startled – the cast, or the firemen confronted by a lot of people in strange costumes and men brandishing swords.

"That story incidentally, is where Gilbert and I met – he was one of the men attending Thomas a Beckett, and had just managed to repel one of the attacking knights when the firemen burst in...I think he thought at first that someone had amended the script!

"The addiction Gilbert and I have to Gilbert and Sullivan operettas is, as they say, well documented! I'll apologise now for boring the pants off some of you with our anecdotes, but we do love them for their humour and their music. After the church incident we were first together on stage in 'The Mikado' with our local Savoyards, and before anyone makes any wisecracks, no, I was not one of the Three Little Maids from School.

"The operettas have given us both such joy and happiness and the opportunity to meet so many talented and lovely people. Four soloists from the D'Oyly Carte opera company joined with us in one special performance for a Festival and when our leading lady lost her voice, their soprano took over the role and without any rehearsing, meeting the cast, or seeing the stage layout etc., gave a perfectly stunning performance in front of a large audience – amazing! Gilbert and I really believe that both listening to music and joining in the singing makes people feel better and happier. With that in mind and," glancing round the room, "in view of our current situation, perhaps you'd all like to join me in a chorus of 'Show me the way to go home'."

There was a stunned silence for about 30 seconds, then, as Susan sat down grinning, there was a burst of laughter and applause.

Who would have thought it? She has them eating out of the palm of her hand, that's cemented a few friendships, I'd say.

There was a buzz in the room as Susan sat down.

Hallelulia, they're talking together – at last. Not the odd sentence, but actual conversations. Best to let them continue for a while, we've still got ages to wait. Then I think a break for milk or tea, as that's all we've got, and see if anyone else has thought of something to say. And I mustn't forget to tell them about Manuel Ronaldo, he's been a dear helpful old soul and in view of his personal circumstances, I think they should be made aware of what he's been through in the last few weeks.

The break over, Hazel found Manuel in the palheiro and taking him by the hand walked with him through the house and into the centre of the group.

"I think it's important you should all know something about our host. His name is Manuel Ronaldo and he has lived here together with his wife, Madeleine, for 5 years.

"She was famous for her wonderful embroidery and also for her second sight, although I'm told some objected to the latter and called her Mad Madeleine because it seemed she really could see into the future. Three weeks ago she died and her body was taken through one of the levadas to the village in the valley, where their two daughters live, so that she could be buried in the churchyard there. Following the funeral , Manuel insisted on coming back to his home to attend to his cows, sort out what he wanted to keep, prior to putting the property on the market.

"He has, I think you'll agree been a most kind and generous host to us, letting us take over his home, at a time when he was grieving. He deserves our heartfelt thanks." The loud applause was followed by people starting to move. First came the ladies, kissing the old man's leathery cheek and the men shaking his hand warmly and patting him on the back and shoulders. Bemused at first by all the attention, he eventually realised what was happening and whilst the tears glittered in his eyes, his grin was as wide as ever.

Hazel suddenly found David at her side and in a low voice he said, "Well done to you too, Hazel. That was a kind thought and this idea of yours about telling anecdotes has really got them all intermingling. You're a surprising lady."

Embarrassed at his compliments, Hazel watched him as he moved away, this time stopping to chat to Madge, who in no time was laughing with him. No doubt charm was necessary in his profession. Consoling and reassuring pets' owners that all would be well, would be an important part of his duties. Was flattering ladies his forte? Was he one of those men who thrived on flirtations but never wanted to take things any further? More importantly, was there a wife, or a significant other, waiting for him at home? Perhaps the next few days would reveal his true nature.

At this point, Alex Moreau got to his feet and at a nod from Hazel, started to speak, stopping everyone in their tracks.

"My mother, Bridget, was a nun." Smothered gasps from around the room.

"At the age of 14 she became pregnant, and in a family of devout Catholics, I can assure you that this was the ultimate sin. She was quickly banished to a Catholic convent which housed a section for girls who had also 'sinned'. The baby was taken away at birth and at her parents' request Bridget was kept in the convent where she was educated and acted as an unpaid worker.

"At 16 years she was transferred to another convent where she was still required to work long hours in the laundry and kitchen, but where she received more education, so that at the age of twenty she was steeped in theology and had developed a love of history. From a French nun, Bridget acquired a familiarity with the language and very soon became immersed in studies about French people and their culture.

"Her request of the Mother Superior that she might join the noviciate with a view to becoming a nun was treated with caution. It had first to be established whether she had any dependants. Had she located the whereabouts of her baby, born all those years ago and followed up the connection? If that had been the case, her request to join holy orders would have been refused. It was not until her 21st birthday that Bridget's acceptance was confirmed. Two years later she was transferred to yet another convent and joined the ranks of the holy sisters there.

"The dreams didn't start until Bridget was in her mid twenties. Dreams of a tiny baby, fleeting glimpses of a head covered with downy black hair, perfect fingers and toes and dark blue eyes, recurred nightly. Soon the dreams began to take over her life, obliterating her devotions to the extent that statues and pictures of the Virgin Mary carrying the holy child soon became pictures of a young girl holding a baby with dark hair and deep blue eyes.

"It was not until her 33rd year that Bridget approached the Mother Superior asking for permission to leave Holy Orders. Again, such a request would not have been treated lightly. When this was finally granted she was offered assistance by the local authority, who suggested that her knowledge of the French language could be used in a translating capacity and that they would be prepared to grant her financial assistance, whilst in training. Within a month she had embarked on a year's training at a local language academy.

"Once that was finished life was, for a time, very hard and she survived by giving extra coaching to children studying French. There was a trickle of translation work but not enough to pay the bills, until someone suggested she write to a publisher of French novels asking for work in translating the books into English. Almost overnight everything changed and she was flooded with work. Now, at last, she could afford the little luxuries for which she had often yearned...decent clothes, a night out at the local theatre, an occasional meal out, but still deep in her heart the one thing she longed for more than anything else was out of her reach, a child. As she approached forty she knew her time was running out.

"Quite deliberately Bridget booked a holiday abroad, determined that she would find someone to sire a child. She intended to be selective, conscious that family genes could affect both appearance and intelligence. To this end she spent a great deal of time in places of academic importance – ancient temples, cathedrals, museums. And it was at one of these she met Dominique.

"He was a tutor at a local college, fifty-one, a widower and intelligent. They were comfortable in each other's company, in fact he ticked all the boxes. Their consummation brought no suggestion of marriage nor was it expected and, as her holiday came to an end, Bridget must have sent up many fervent prayers that her dream had been fulfilled.

"Since childhood Bridget had been a loner and her life in the convents had exacerbated this, but there was one factor of which no-one but she was aware and it would not leave her – desperation to give birth again and to keep the child. Her search for a suitable man to father her child had been quite deliberate and she was not surprised when having found him, he had showed no interest in giving up his life in France to share hers in the UK.

"Her prayers were answered, pregnancy confirmed, and because of her age, she was now turned 40, concerned staff decided to move her into hospital early, feeling she needed maximum supervision. I was of course, that baby and, I am happy to say, blessed with the most loving and considerate of mothers. Soon she was able to resume her work from home as a translator and together we lived happily for some five years, when fate took an unexpected turn of events.

"My father, Dominique, arrived at our home one Friday evening and announced that he felt it was time that he and my mother were married. Leaving behind him his academic life-style was clearly hard, but in Bridget and me he had a family, something he had never previously experienced. No longer a young man, he was aware, realistically, that this might be his salvation in the years to come. My parents' lives together can only be described as chequered, my mother strong-willed with long established firm opinions and my father used to being obeyed in the classroom and to having peace and quiet when he wished to study. In spite of their ups and downs, their pride when I went to university was wonderful to behold.

"Sadly they are neither of them with us now, but my own experience of a life filled with love has set the feet of Marie and myself on unexpected pathways where we can sometimes pass this on to others. But I will leave her to explain what I mean by that.

Thank you".

There were murmurs of approval and Hazel crossed over to where Marie was sitting to ask her if she and

Alex would remain close to Driver Jo's bedside, as and when the goods were dropped onto the promontory. From what Alex had said the two of them were the most experienced to administer whatever was sent, ensuring that if Jo had to be taken off by a winch, he would be fully sedated. David was next on her list. Her mobile would not last indefinitely and she must ensure she had access to another and give that number to the police.

Motioning to David and Jack, together the three of them left the house to survey the outside scene. The mist had thinned in different areas and they could now see the exact edge of the promontory, probably 10 to 12 metres beyond the house, the land tapering at its rear another 15 metres. To one side of the palheiro there was a wider stretch of about 20 metres to the promontory edge, extending to a further 20 to 40 metres behind it. They now saw that the shifting mist had left a clearance over the promontory, but would it be sufficient?

Jack's comment was "It will depend on the amount of clarity above the mist and, fingers crossed, there is a glimmer of sunshine behind us, so hopefully, we'll be O.K."

There were anxious faces at the window and a group started to filter outside. Again came the warning from David, "Stay close to the house, please."

Manuel was the next to appear from the palheiro. He smiled and said something in Portuguese, which no-one understood, then a wave of relief passed through the group as he raised his thumbs and nodded his head.

He must surely know the weather better than anyone, I hope to God he's right.

David's phone rang and the smiles faded as he handed it over to Hazel with a serious expression. What now?

"Hello yes, are you able to come?"

"Miss Godwin, this is the position. As you can see there's still a lot of mist around, but it's clear enough above it for us to drop all your requirements. What we feel we must also attempt, and much will depend on visibility, is to take your injured driver off the site.

"To do this we will first drop your requirements as central to the area behind the palheiro as possible. The scientists advise us not to land there as the thrust of the rotors and the down draught might in themselves disturb the solidity of the ravine face. Whilst I know your people would be intrigued to watch all this, you'll appreciate we cannot have many people moving in that area which again might cause land tremors. Please arrange that just 2 to 3 men are detailed off to come and collect your food etc. Please also ask Manuel to put out the tarpaulin which he once painted white and laid in the middle of the area behind the palheiro. It is a good marker for our people on this sort of exercise.

"With regard to your driver, we will first of all drop our sling which is more of a structured cradle to hold someone injured, under its straps are 2 blankets. Our winch man will accompany it. Whoever opens the boxes already lowered will find at the very top a box marked with a cross – this contains a strong sedative which one of your members must administer to the patient at once. Two of your men under the supervision of the winch man will then strap the driver into the cradle and carry him outside. Don't worry if you can't hear us overhead for a few minutes, we have direct contact with the winch man. Once we know that the patient is secure we will be overhead and lower the cable and the patient and our winch man will be raised together.

"I am so sorry that we cannot do more at the moment but we have to accept that the area has been badly disrupted and the ground might still be volatile. Tomorrow we will again review the weather situation and if there is an improvement we are considering bringing in another helicopter and lifting off all your people in batches.

"I think we will find that Manuel wishes to stay with his cows and property until further arrangements can be made, so we will ensure sufficient food is also left for him.

"We will contact you later when your driver has safely reached the hospital and we would remind you that tonight there will be a spectacular firework display. Whilst you will not be able to witness it in the comfort we might have hoped, your vantage point will be second to none. Just remind people to stay very close to the house. Any other questions Miss Godwin?"

"No, thank you – I think you've just about covered everything – thank you again."

***

Chapter 4

The drone of the helicopter sent them all crowding to the windows. First of all in a light-weight wooden structure were their foodstuffs, etc. Quickly the men took that into the house and Marie and Alex found the medical supplies at the top as promised.

The pack containing a syringe and sedative was used and within seconds Jo was sound asleep. The winch man arrived with the cradle and together they lifted Jo, wrapping him in one blanket, strapping him in and covering him with a further hood and blanket. Then he and the winch man were soon being transported heavenward, a sight which made them all feel emotional.

Hazel quickly diverted their attention to opening the boxes which had arrived.

"Right team, let's see what we've got to eat – I'm starving!"

There were exclamations of delight as they uncovered boxes of cooked chicken breasts, slices of ham, cartons of soup, wedges of cheese, quiches, bread rolls, butter, cakes and puddings galore, fresh fruit, some carefully packed bottles of wine, even paper plates, cups, napkins and plastic cutlery. "It's a veritable feast!" exclaimed Susan and they all agreed. Without more ado both the table and the top of the ottoman was used to spread everything out and they were soon all busily eating and expressing delight at having such a substantial meal.

Hazel's mind was racing ahead as to how to fill the hours before the fireworks started at approximately 10.0p.m. *It will be fine, if the others are prepared to tell their own stories, if not, it could be another long haul.* Just as she was worrying about it, Jack came over and said "I've got a story and I know that Marie is also ready to follow up what Alex said and talk about where they're at now."

"Thanks Jack, as soon as the decks are cleared of food, we'll start again."

It was five o'clock when they at last had the seating arranged again and without more ado Marie moved her chair forward so that she could see everyone.

"Alex has told you something of our background and his ancestry. You can now understand why we have a French surname and why he is bilingual. Several amongst you have asked if I was a nurse and the answer to that is 'Yes, we both were'. We met whilst training in Paris and became, as they say today, 'an item'. We married in our early 20's and decided to work in the UK because Alex's mother was still alive and living on her own. To our regret we have no children and this is I think what triggered the next stage of our lives. We both found work in London at St. Thomas's hospital and by the age of 28 held the ranks of senior staff nurse and sister in charge. Increasingly horrified at the havoc caused by natural disasters throughout the world and the plight of the children affected by them we asked the hospital for permission to enrol with the Médicins Sans Frontières. Obviously this had to be approved because it would mean that in an emergency we would have to leave for the disaster zone as soon as possible, with the inevitable disruption to the hospital staffing rotas. Approval was given and since then we have been called to assist in many areas throughout the world, never anticipating that one day we would be dealing with our own disaster.

"Always we have been overwhelmed by the numbers of missing children left behind. and horrified by the amount of people who even in the most dire situations manage to infiltrate the scene in order to acquire children and exploit them. We have now come to a decision that although we're both 50, when we return home we are going to start the adoption procedure - latterly there has seemed to be a relaxation of some of the rules regarding mixed race adoption and adoptive parents' ages, so we are hopeful.

"We know that with the example of Alex's mother, we can give a child a caring and loving home. I wish there could have been more we could do for Driver Jo, but without the opportunity to X-Ray and with no medicines we have just attempted to keep him as comfortable as possible and we do thank you all for your continued assistance with that."

Again ripples of applause and murmurs of approval all round.

Goodness, this is a different and unexpected side to Marie. Even when she was helping Jo, I thought her rather stand-offish. Now I can see she was probably desperately worried that she couldn't do more. Another lesson learned. Don't judge a book by its cover – she and Alex must have witnessed some horrendous situations

Perhaps that makes you more self-contained, certainly it would make you less likely to waste words on flippancy and nonsense. Now the girls are embracing her and she's really top of the pops. Who would have thought it? Jack, bless him, has already moved his chair forward – I'd better say something.

"Thank you, Marie. I think we're all staggered that we have a couple amongst us who have witnessed the aftermath of the natural disasters the rest of us only see on television. It almost goes without saying that we admire your bravery and wish you and Alex well with regard to adoption – I'm sure no child could wish for a better home. Now, I think our friend from across the seas in Oz has a story to tell us."

Jack grinned at them and then began.

"This is my grandfather's story which was handed down to his son and from him to me. My granddad was born in the East End of London to a single mother whose life revolved around finding a series of 'Uncles' to bring home for the night. Grandad Jack rarely had enough to eat and when the London air raids started during the 2nd World War his mother was quick to put his name on a list for evacuation. He left home with a brown paper carrier bag carrying an old shirt to wear in bed, a pair of socks, a gas mask and a jam sandwich.

"Arriving in the West Country he was lucky to be taken to the home of a farmer, his wife and family of three children. They were horrified at the boy's half starved appearance and lack of clothing, the absence of a ration book, identity card and clothing coupons, but soon set on a mission to put things right. Subtly they introduced him to proper eating habits, using their own coupons to buy pyjamas and decent trousers and sweaters. When it was his birthday and Mrs. C. made a cake with lighted candles his expression of wonderment had all of them tearful. He loved life on the farm, got up early to see the farmer milking, and started to thrive and do well at school.

"There was never any communication from his mother. At the end of the war when children were being returned home, the WVS, Red Cross and other organisations found it impossible to trace her, coming to the conclusion that she must have died in an air raid. Much as his family at the farm would have loved to keep Jack, Mrs. C. was pregnant and knew she couldn't manage with five children and the work of a farmer's wife, so, reluctantly, he was put in an orphanage for boys, run by Catholics. It was a case of survival of the fittest. The food was poor and the bigger boys stole from the smaller ones, to such an extent they were all on the point of suffering from malnutrition.

"Life was hard and when, after two years, a man came to the orphanage promising them a new life in a wonderful new country all the boys were excited. They were told they would be adopted in Australia and go to new homes. Jack was very hopeful that he would be as fortunate as he had been in the West Country and go to live with another lovely family. Twenty-five boys were chosen and soon they were on the dockside at Southampton ready to board a ship. Photos were taken of them holding the toys handed out, but Jack noticed that as soon as the newsmen disappeared, the toys disappeared too.

"It was a long journey to Freemantle in Western Australia, but the boys were fed better than they had been for a long time and excited at what lay ahead. On arrival they were met by two men in long black garments, who called themselves Christian Brothers. The children were quickly shepherded onto the waiting coach and from there driven north of Perth until they came to Bindoon, the home of the Christian Brothers. They were told to wash their hands and return to the main hall for food and sit at the long tables there. The eldest amongst them was eleven and a half, the youngest four and a half.

"A man called Brother Kendrick spoke and welcomed them to Bindoon and said they were very lucky because they were going to be part of a project to complete the building and its surrounds. Nothing at all about them being adopted which they'd been promised. The boys thought Brother Kendrick must have got it wrong because they were told the next morning to wear their thinnest, lightest clothes, pyjamas if necessary, as they would be building and it would be very hot. Puzzled they whispered to each other that this must be a mistake. How could they be building? Most were too little anyway and none of them knew anything at all about building. The next morning they were roused by a bell very early and told to wash and dress and make their beds. Little Joe, just four, had wet his bed and Jack, my Grandad, said he was shocked at the way one of the Brothers spoke to him, calling him a pig who deserved to lie in his own muck. Jack and his friend Brian took care of Little Joe and spread the bed sheets and mattress out to dry near the window.

"It took the boys a while to work out just how their meals were planned. For breakfast they had two sausages, fried egg, two slices of bread and butter and a mug of tea. It took them a while to realise that they had to be fed properly at the beginning of the day, otherwise they would be unable to work. They were shown how to mix cement and to build walls according to the lines of cord, marking where they should be. As the walls got higher they were to leave that section to dry off, (quickly in that heat) and then small ladders could be used to complete them to a height of six feet.

"It was when another friend told them about a visit from one of the Brothers late at night that things deteriorated. Grandad had seen animals being mated at the farm so he was not unfamiliar with matters of that nature, but at first could hardly believe that a religious man of the church could have behaved as their friend had told them. Soon it became obvious that this was not a one off affair. Boys would be taken from the dormitory during the night and brought back stunned and crying. Several times boys had to be hospitalised, but still the Brothers were not reported for their assaults on these young, vulnerable children.

"Grandad was sixteen when he planned his escape. He had noticed that a lorry which came regularly with bricks and cement had a boy about his age with the driver. During the morning break he managed to talk to the boy and asked if he would help.

"People in the immediate community had been told they would be punished if they assisted escapees, so Carl was wary. However, he said their final trip was in two weeks' time, when his boss would be retiring. Jack asked if Carl could get him any clothes and shoes. He had never had a pair of shoes since he left the UK. Carl said he'd do what he could and on the planned date during the morning break, Jack waited for the right moment and then slipped under the canvas at the back of the lorry and soon they were off. Approaching Freemantle the lorry stopped and Jack was given a bag with his clothes, a pair of plimsolls, a bottle of water and some apples and told he was on his own.

"At a nearby farm a girl hid him in the barn, gave him more food and, more importantly, the address of her uncle, a builder, in Freemantle. She told Jack her uncle was a good man and he would be safe there. And he was. The builder and his wife took him in and he became like a son to them. He joined the building firm under an assumed name and after some years married their niece, the girl who had helped him during his escape and together they eventually inherited the firm. They were, of course, my grandparents.

"My grandfather had been introduced to bowls by the builder who had taken him in and it was during a match against a visiting touring side of policemen that he met one of the visitors and told him about Bindoon. He also told the policeman that he thought the Brothers must have changed his birth certificate. He'd always been known as Jack but in the transfer to Bindoon he was suddenly addressed as Reg. The policeman asked if he could remember anyone in the East End where he had lived and Jack said there was an old man who had a fruit and veg. stall there who had often given him fruit at the end of the day. He couldn't remember the man's name and in any event so many years had passed the man would probably be dead by now.

"Two weeks later, to his amazement, he received a letter from the UK, saying the policeman had found out exactly where he came from and yes, his name *was* Jack and his birth certificate had been changed. In the East End the old man's son had been tracked down and did remember him, saying he thought Jack's mother had gone off with a serviceman. Finally, through the NHS, the policeman was able to tell him that whilst his mother was dead, he had a sister who lived in America and had now been informed of his existence.

"The happy ending is that the two families made contact and became firm friends.

"The not so happy ending is that many of the children who were sent abroad at the same time as Grandad, were never able to find out where their roots were and for the rest of their lives felt they had been cheated. One boy said to Jack, "They told me my folks had died in a car crash. We never had no car and I don't think there's any way we would have had one, ever. They definitely changed my name on the birth certificate."

"Like Alex, I have been fortunate in being surrounded by a loving family. I have worked hard to ensure that my Grandfather's building firm continued to thrive and now" grinning, "at the ripe old age of thirty four, feel it's time I started a family of my own. I've just spent a week in America and, sort of hoped, I might meet the girl of my dreams, but it was not to be. So, ladies, I'm footloose and fancy free –if anyone is interested!"

With that and to a wave of applause, Jack sat down.

What a wonderful man he is. I doubt he'll be unattached for very long. He obviously loved his grandfather a great deal and is full of admiration for the way he survived a horrendous experience. He runs a business and the speed with which he dealt with our nightmare accident was amazing. He took control but without in any way being overbearing. Just quietly went about getting us all organised. Had we all panicked and rushed around, I dread to think what might have happened. He's probably looking for someone in their twenties so I don't imagine I'd even get off first base. But how I wish…… Just time for another speaker, should be a female really, but David's already signalling, so I'd better give him the go ahead.

"David…..Yes, by all means, if you're ready."

"Several of you have asked if there have been any unusual incidents in my work as a vet. Yes, there have been a multitude – I'd like to tell you about one or two in a moment, but perhaps I could first of all add something to Jack's fascinating story about his grandfather's experiences. I recently read a book by the woman who uncovered this can of worms. She was asked by someone in Australia to try and trace his parents in the UK and found some disconcerting threads in his background. His birth certificate had also been changed and there were other discrepancies. She put out a message on radio in Australia asking for anyone who had been sent out there for 'a new life' after the 2nd World War, to get in touch with her. She expected about 100 callers, in fact there were over 2,000.

"Questions to the Foreign Office about these children who were shipped out to Canada, Australia and Rhodesia were ignored – it seemed no-one wanted to talk about them. Then one morning she found a parcel on her doorstep consisting of a number of files outlining the numbers deported from orphanages with this same promise of a new life. The most disturbing of all was that from Rhodesia, where the government stipulated that they wanted only white children and of superior intelligence. Clearly the idea was to create a super-structure of intelligent whites to keep the coloured population under control – disgusting.

"At last she was able to disclose just what had been happening to the boys at Bindoon and elsewhere, and Australia went into shock at the news, having always prided themselves on being generous in spirit and hospitality.

"A friend of mine went out to Perth recently and travelled north to Bindoon. Outside the complex is a huge statue of Brother Kendrick with his arms round the shoulders of two boys. As my friend looked upwards a voice behind him said, 'Someone ought to have put a bomb under this place years ago'. I can tell you however, that Bindoon is no longer the home of the Christian Brothers, it is now an Agricultural College. I know from my own meetings with Australians the knowledge is a thorn in the side of all Australians who know of the horrors of what went on there.

"Now, to my work. Yes, I have operated on lions, rhinos and very many other animals, having lived for a time in South Africa and India, in addition, of course, to the usual assortment of household pets. I used to like going into schools to talk to the children about my experiences. Probably the smallest animal on which I've operated was a pet mouse – it had a tumour which I was able to remove. Then there was a cat which had clearly attacked a bird and devoured it before becoming ill. The cat stopped eating and drinking was losing weight daily and it was not until it was very ill that I found that it had a 6 inch long feather wrapped tightly around its bronchial tube which was stopping it from ingesting food. Sadly it was too late to save it.

"The most frightening experience I have had in my work was a call from a zoo saying that two of their big and dangerous snakes had been fighting, were now lying at the bottom of the cage immobile and someone had to go in and find out if they were dead or alive. And yes, that someone was me. In fact I found that one was dead and the other had broken its back – yes, snakes do have vertebrae, and it had to be put down.

"The last question from one class was interesting. I was asked by a boy, 'Have you ever operated on a fish, Sir?' my reply was 'Only with a knife and fork!'"

To a gale of laughter, David concluded and Hazel checked her watch.

Just time now for them to have a drink and a snack, prepare their beds for later and then wrap up warmly ready for going out to see the firework display.

"Thank you to all our story tellers this afternoon and evening. I think we might now prepare the drinks ready to herald in the New Year, have a hot drink prior to going outside and it will help if we get our beds ready too, so that when the display is finished we can come in and settle down straight away. We have no set time for departure tomorrow – it could well be that we'll be once again waiting for the sun to burn off the fog, but I think we must be prepared just in case they arrive earlier than planned. If we have to wait then I'm hopeful that those of you who haven't yet spoken to us, might have come up with something.

"Just a further reminder, the safety of our group members is paramount. *No-one*, *repeat no-one*, is to go anywhere near the edge of the promontory. All being well the helicopter will land and depart from the middle of the open area behind the palheiro. As soon as we have an arrival time for the helicopter, I will put a notice on the table saying the order in which we'll be leaving. I can tell you now that we feel it is important that Sally and Tom leave first. The police force have organised doctors to go to Reid's and check us all for any problems, but I'm sure you'll agree that Sally must

68

take priority."

Murmurs of assent, then sudden activity as the plastic glasses and the wine Reid's had sent were set out on the table. Dishes of crisps and nuts appeared as if by magic and a large box of chocolates They each prepared their beds and ensured their handbags or small holdalls were packed. The kettle was set on the brazier, a jug of milk, plastic cups and the box of tea bags were all in pole position ready for the off.

I never know whether to laugh or cry. It's like we're all playing dolls' houses again, but I'm sure this is something the trauma team will be very interested in – the fact that in the most bizarre of circumstances we still fall back on the habits of a lifetime as if desperate to recreate what we currently haven't got.

At 7.30 p.m. the phone rang. David's battery was now run down, so this time it was Jack who came to hand the mobile over so that Hazel could talk to the police.

"Sorry, Miss Godwin, it's the same as before I'm afraid. Unless the weather takes a rapid turn for the better, the meteorologists think the fog won't be sufficiently burned off before about 12.30 or 1.0 p.m. We have organised two helicopters. I understand you have a lady with a well advanced pregnancy?"

"Yes, that's right."

"Then, I'm sure you'll agree that she and her husband should be first to leave. The doctors will want to spend more time with her. The rest of the rota I leave to you. The winch man is always with the pilot and he will land to ensure that people board safely, don't get near the rotors, that sort of thing. Is there anything else?"

"Only that I would like to leave last, please. And could you stay on the line and explain all this to Manuel. Most of what we say has to be done by sign

69

language, so he'd appreciate talking to you."

"No problem. I'll look forward to seeing you tomorrow. Enjoy the fireworks."

Signals to Manuel and the phone duly handed over to him, the few precious chairs were brought outside so that Sally and anyone else wanting to sit down, might watch in comfort . Then Hazel suggested that they put on warm jackets and bring out some blankets, ready for the chill night air. Whilst they were doing that she sat down with Jack and drew up the list of the order of departure. Sally and Tom with the eldest couple Susan and Gilbert first, Johann and Rachel with Madge next, Alex, Marie, and Jane, with Colin, David, Jack and herself last. Jack was in agreement with Hazel that it made sense if the three men remained with her, just in case there proved to be any items requiring manhandling. He accepted without question Hazel's insistence that she left last, as correct.

At midnight exactly, a rocket soared into the night sky to be followed by explosion after explosion of brilliant, shimmering colours. Together they ooh'd and aah'd as each new masterpiece of creativity appeared against the backdrop of the dark blue sky. How they laughed when suddenly a huge screen bade a welcome to 'Our stranded visitors to Funchal.' In the distance they could see the ships at sea – and it was left to their imagination to picture those ships with their huge floral displays, bottles of Madeira wine being poured into crystal glasses and cruise passengers in full evening dress. Now vast screens accompanied by music showed folk dancing and all amidst showers of multi-coloured stars lighting up the coast line. The circumstances were not what they had expected, but it was reassuring. Yes, it was tantalisingly close but it gave them a feeling of contact with the outside world. And that helped to temporarily put out of their minds the horror they had experienced and the knowledge that they were not out of danger yet.

In a strange way it's a balm for all of us, after a period in which we've been traumatised by fear and the bleakness of shortage of food and most of all, not being able to just sit down and cry at the unfairness of it all. All of us, me included, came here for a period of relaxation, some sunshine and beauty, contrasting with the routine of work at home and wintry weather. Instead we have been faced with containing our emotions, worrying about other people and hoping and praying that someone would come and rescue us as soon as possible. Like children we have tonight been fed on this feast of beauty and left in awe and wonderment. Now we can grit our teeth and face another few hours with the promise of normality sometime tomorrow.

The chairs returned to the house, the wine poured, they gathered together in the limited space available and raised their glasses to each other.

They're all thinking of where they were last year – probably with families or even at New Year's Eve Balls. Never imagining in their wildest possible imaginations that this year they might be stranded somewhere near the top of a mountain with a group of people they had only just got to know. But we could have been killed – all of us. So perhaps they're sending up fervent prayers to thank whoever's up there that, with the exception of Jo, we're all in pretty good condition. Poor old Manuel was no doubt remembering that his wife had been with him at this time last year, but he still managed that warm-hearted gummy grin as different members of the group patted him on the shoulders or, in the case of the women, embraced and kissed him.

I feel absolutely exhausted, I don't know about the

rest of the group but I for one am well ready for Reid's administrations, I need cosseting, feeding and want to sleep in a decent bed for at least 12 hours. Roll on tomorrow!!

***

Chapter 5

8.0 a.m. the next day and everyone was washed, hair combed and after toast held over the brazier and a hot cup of tea, seemed ready to face the world. Just a few of the palettes were left in the main room. These together with the few chairs and the ottoman would provide places for them to sit during the next few hours.

I don't want to put them under any pressure, but perhaps those who haven't spoken might be happy to do so. I can only ask.

"Is there anyone who hasn't spoken who wants to do so. It's entirely up to you…."

Rachel Landau raised her hand immediately.

"Hazel, Johann and I have talked about this and I would like to tell you something of our background. As you will have gathered from our names, we are Jews. This again is a story relayed to us by our grandparents, I'm afraid. Johann has said many times that neither of us thought of ourselves first and foremost as Jews. We regarded the homeland where we were born as the most important thing about us – Hans, whose grandfather was an Austrian and my grandmother, Margot, who was Polish. Our Jewishness is our religion and not our nationality.

"Margot left Poland in her teens to go to university in Berlin, where she met and later married Hans. As the Nazi attitude to the Jews in Berlin became more unpredictable, they saw elderly Jews being made to scrub the Berlin streets and received very disturbing news from Margot's Polish family. Hans, alarmed at the growing aggression to Jews by the Nazi regime, suggested they should prepare to leave the country. Their furniture crated, they started to make plans.

"By this time Margot was working as a governess at

a private house, whilst Hans had a job at their old university. One evening he met Margot from work and told her that the Jewish shops in the ghetto had been set alight by the S.S. and that they must leave at once. She asked when and his answer was 'I'm afraid, my darling, I mean just that. We will leave tomorrow!"

"Hans found it hard to believe that Austrians whom he had always believed to be a proud and upright race, welcoming visitors to their country, were suddenly becoming so pro-Nazi. A speech by Adolf Hitler in one of the squares had attracted large crowds enthusiastically saluting him. There was no time for being fussy about packing or extended goodbyes, the next day they left and just one week after their departure, Hitler closed the gates of Nazi Germany with no-one allowed either in or out. Fortunately, by this time Hans and Margot had arrived safely in the United Kingdom.

" Once they had found accommodation in the U.K. Hans managed to get a job in a munitions factory which made bomb noses. He became friendly with one of the women there, Rita Baker, and soon he took his wife Margot to meet her. Rita was separated from her husband. She had three children and had been drafted into the munitions factory from a woollen mill. She and the other women there had to learn how to use a capstan lathe to an accuracy of 1 millimetre in two months – normally an apprentice would be learning this trade for a period of three years. Rita told my grandmother Margot, that Hans got quite agitated when the factory men stopped working to have a cigarette or a cup of tea. He always said to them "If you had seen what we've seen, you would keep working non stop, doing anything to prevent that devil getting a hold on your country."

"At the end of the war our grandparents tried

through various agencies to trace their families. The whole of Margot's family had disappeared into the holocaust without trace – her parents, 3 brothers, and 2 sisters, she probably having been the only one to escape. Just what happened to them we will never know. Either they were sent along with many thousands of others by train to concentration camps, or they were victims of one of the ghetto massacres, when once the ghetto was packed with people, the gates were closed and there was systematic killing of those inside.

"Hans was more fortunate in his searching. The agency tracked down his brother who had also escaped from Germany and managed to get to the USA. After the war Hans and Margot went to the States to join his brother and family and they stayed there for the rest of their lives. My own mother, Hazel Paula, was born there. I met Johann at work in California, we were both solicitors and following our marriage we promised ourselves a visit to the UK where our grandparents had been made so welcome.

"This year we have done just that, taken an extended holiday, travelled all over the UK and before returning to the USA decided to have a nice relaxing holiday on this beautiful island before resuming work. It hasn't quite worked out as planned… but on the credit side we have met some lovely people who we trust will be our friends for life. We certainly are hopeful that you will come and visit us once we are at home in California… not all at once of course. Always the world seems to be wracked by troubles, often with its roots in greed. If we can play a part, however small, in healing old wounds and showing that people of different creeds and from different backgrounds can still be good friends, then we feel we will have in some small part helped to ease the world's wounds. Thank you."

Rachel's audience looked stunned for a few

moments, then there were enthusiastic ripples of approval and clapping.

Well, good for her. A difficult subject when there's always trouble in the Middle East, but she presented her case without prejudice and with enough background to give everyone a great deal to think about. Anyone else, I wonder? Great, Madge is on her feet. Wonderful, in spite of my fears, so many of them have grasped the nettle and found something to tell the rest of us about. Time to comment and introduce Madge.

"Thank you, Rachel. I think I can speak for everyone when I say we are all saddened that throughout the world, wars continue to erupt and it's difficult to equate these with the fact that so often they're generated by differences of religion. It's good for all of us, even in a small group such as ours, to consider the evil which has from time to time erupted and to play our own part by respecting the different beliefs of our friends. Now, I think Madge is next in the pipeline. Madge…?

"Like Susan, I too, have been involved with drama for most of my life. It started in school when I was lucky enough to get a part in the play 'The Barretts of Wimpole Street' – I absolutely loved it and the seed was sown. From there it was a short step to taking some lessons and joining a drama society.

"When I was in my early twenties a request came via my former Youth Club leader, a JP, that I take part with the prisoners at a high security prison nearby, in their Christmas play. My parents were less than keen with the idea, but I felt it was an experience not to be missed. The first rehearsal was in a Nissen hut sited in the middle of the prison grounds. There were two prison wardens seated outside and the cast, all men of course, seemed friendly enough – one even said it was very kind of my parents to let me take part with them!

"As we approached the prison for the second rehearsal, the producer, a local man, said, 'The Governor has come to give you the once over'. I was quite alarmed, but sure enough at the Prison gates was an elderly man with silver hair who shook my hand and wished me well. I then found the security was different from the first week, with two wardens outside and one inside – I wasn't quite sure what to construe from that!

"There was only one 'incident' during rehearsals. One of the players forgot his words and another man, who I later found was in for Grievous Bodily Harm, lost his temper and was on the point of striking out – fortunately the warden intervened. The prisoners were a mixed bunch. One young man with a crystal cut accent had been trained at Sandhurst and was an army officer – apparently he'd been helping himself to army funds.

"The play was set in a village pub and I was the landlady, the only female. My one moment of real nervousness was when I was taken by a Trustee down a long corridor to the Prison Education Officer's office to change into my costume. The sound of the key turning in the lock and the man's receding footsteps made me suddenly realise that I was in the middle of a high security prison – on my own!

"The play was to be shown in the gymnasium which was the nearest point to the outside wall, so security there was extra tight. There were wardens stationed in the wings at the far side of the stage and we members of the cast could only use the other wing, plus a central door at the rear of the set. The audience of prisoners were in the main well of the hall and on each side was a very wide section running down to the stage area – seated all the way down the centre of each side section was a line of wardens, one in front of the others, so that the prisoners were completely ringed. At the rear of the hall were the VIPs, the Governor, Deputy Governor, senior officers and their wives.

"The Prison Officer whose office I had been using to change into my stage clothes, was quite a formidable man. About 6ft. 7in. in height with broad shoulders, he had a 'No nonsense' manner written all over him. Just before the curtains were due to rise on the play, he strode onto the apron of the stage, still wearing his very large mackintosh, what used to be called a rider's mac. Unfastened at the front, it billowed out behind him and at the sides, making him look even bigger and more formidable than ever. Stopping in the middle of the stage, feet apart, he glared at the prisoners and said in a loud, clear voice, "Now lads, tonight we have a lady in the cast. I want no bad language and no catcalls – is that quite clear?" There was a shuffling of feet and a low murmuring which could have been interpreted in any way you wished and then he strode off the stage and the play began.

"What surprised me more than anything was the, to me, unexpected reaction of the prisoners to certain phrases. 'He's just gone outside' and anything involving the word 'free', produced ripples of laughter and applause. Behind the curtains, at the end of the show, I was given flowers and chocolates and one of the cast made a nice little speech thanking me for taking part. For me, the whole thing proved an unforgettable experience.

"I know you'll all be aware of the success of Agatha Christie's mysteries and her name on a poster advertising a play still draws people in great numbers to see it. Sadly, some of the scripted versions of the books are not quite so well written as they might be. In one I had to go on stage and look out onto the balcony where a man was slumped forward in a wheel-chair with a knife in his back right up to the hilt. My line was "Is he dead?" As he couldn't have appeared more dead if he'd tried, I just couldn't say this without wanting to giggle. Inevitably I was joined by the corpse and the other person on stage. The Director agreed it was an awful line in the circumstances and allowed me to modify it to "Oh, no! Is he REALLY dead?" Still not brilliant, but it curbed the giggles.

"On the first Saturday of one of my own productions, 'Wind in the Willows', having played the matinee to a packed house, we all adjourned to our separate bases for tea and a brief respite before the evening performance. Then the phone rang to say the theatre was on fire and the fire brigade was there – action stations all round. At the theatre we found, thankfully, that most of the damage was under the stage where a large group of teenagers had had to change. Fortunately the caretaker's wife had seen a plume of smoke from under the stage door, just as she and her husband were locking up. They rang for help and the brigade quickly dealt with the problem.

"Under the stage, a large pile of velvet curtains was destroyed, as were a number of costumes, this meant I had to make a quick dash to our rehearsal rooms where the company's wardrobe was housed. Back at the theatre, costumes were handed over and the cast members were assured that everything was now OK. We didn't tell the audience there had been a fire until the final curtain came down and they were full of admiration that in spite of the initial panic, all had gone smoothly. The source of the trouble? We had our suspicions that some of our youngsters might have thought tucked away under the stage was a good place to have a crafty cigarette!

"Several months later, a second fire incident started in the floors above our basement rehearsal rooms. These floors housed a departmental store and the prime suspect was the restaurant on the top floor. At 11.0 p.m. one night I had a phone call to say our premises were on fire. As Club President that year I had a set of keys and drove quickly to the area. The High Street was cordoned off and it was obvious that the fire had already spread downwards. I managed to find a senior officer and handed over the keys to our rooms, explaining that the basement housed antique furniture and artefacts, plus a large amount of valuable period costumes. He promised his men would do what they could to save them.

"The worst moment was at midnight having to phone the owner, who had moved some distance away from our area. It was he who had so kindly always allowed us to use the basement – having to tell him the whole building was on fire, was not easy.

"We were, in fact, very lucky – a beautiful chaise longue and matching armchair had to be recovered and a carpet replaced because of water damage, but we were covered by insurance. The thickness of the basement wall and the fact that our costume wardrobe was sited in an inner chamber resulted in smoke damage being restricted to just a few items. A new departmental store is now in place over our basement, which still houses a great deal of theatrical paraphernalia.

"Like Susan and Gilbert I have, down the years, gained so much pleasure through the theatre, both drama and musicals and experienced the joy of long-lasting friendships. On a different level, I do feel that having together experienced a dramatic experience we, as a group, have benefited in becoming closer to our fellow travellers. Just as, in wartime, people bonded together for the common cause. For me this is the ideal time to say thank you to you all, for your support and friendship."

The smiles of approval were genuine and Hazel was not surprised to find Jack suddenly at her side.

"You're a clever girl, you know that? You've got them all talking and let's face it when we first arrived many of us were as unlike as chalk and cheese. Now, here they are handing out compliments to each other, as if they were going out of fashion."

Hazel blushed, aware she didn't do that very often. "Don't forget your own input. You were brilliant on that first night and I think they still regard you as a leader."

"Don't kid yourself. If there's a problem they turn to you; when they want instructions as to what to do next, they turn to you. You were given this group to take into the great unknown as their leader and travel guide and you've fulfilled your duties to the letter. You do realise of course, they're going to expect a story from you?"

"Oh, help! Surely not?"

"Come on, fair's fair. If they can do it, you certainly can. But I think we've got two more already waiting in the wings, young Colin's on his feet and he's got a piece of paper at the ready and even Jane looks as if she's gearing herself up for the off."

Unusually, Colin was clearly nervous and cleared his throat before starting. Then he held up the paper and said, "Some years ago I asked my grandfather if he would write down some of his experiences. He was a great raconteur and I knew if I relied on my own memory, I might forget something important. So, sorry folks, mine's also a story from a grandparent, but I think you'll understand when you hear it, that I wanted to ensure that I had all the facts right. Having listened to Rachel, I think she and Johann will find this of particular interest. So these are my grandfather's own words. Picking up his sheets of paper, Colin began,

"I joined the Royal Navy as a naval cadet, two

months before my 16th birthday. I trained in Portsmouth at H.M.S. Vincent. From the start it was a hard life. Each morning before breakfast we had to go up and over the mast – that was the rigging of a square rigger which was permanently in the main courtyard outside our headquarters. I personally don't like heights, but somehow I managed to keep that fear under control and do what was necessary. We did have occasions when young lads, particularly newcomers, turned green when they got to the top and had to have assistance in getting back to terra firma.

"Discipline was strict. If you stepped out of line you would be struck on the back of the calves by a stonika, a sort of truncheon held by the Instructor. That was very painful and you didn't get into trouble again in a hurry. There were other surprises when we put to sea. One captain was always seasick as soon as we got outside the Solent. Ratings who were regularly sick were put in the ventilators on deck with a blanket, a bottle of water and ship's dry biscuits. There they stayed, having been told to eat the biscuits, otherwise if they were violently seasick, the lining of the stomach was in danger of tearing. By eating, the stomach had something to reject without serious damage. Now and again someone would go up top and check up on each of them.

"Every morning our beds and lockers were checked for neatness, everything had to be folded and put in its place. One boy who joined the ship was reluctant to wash himself so we boys got together to decide what to do. The next day when he came off duty he was carried bodily to the washing area and dumped, fully clothed, in a bath full of cold water. When he emerged, coughing and spluttering, he was told in no uncertain terms that if he was found unwashed and with stinking socks again, this would be repeated. He soon got the message.

"We all quickly learned that much of the discipline was for our own safety and comfort. We played quite a lot of sport, learned how to handle the tenders which would take us from the sea anchor to the shore and how to take care of ourselves hygienically and attend to the washing of our own personal clothing.

"It was when I was approaching my nineteenth birthday towards the end of 1948 and early in 1949 that I was involved in something which eventually became a blot on Britain's naval history. The end of World War II had resulted in many thousands of Jews trying to get back to their chosen land, Palestine. This was now a British Protectorate and also the Mecca of the Jewish religion. These thousands consisted of those who had been lucky enough to survive the concentration camps and also the many who had been trapped, and often hidden, in occupied countries. They were non-military, displaced people, who believed that if they could get to Palestine they would be safe in the hands of the British people.

"Unfortunately, the British Government realised that if the Jews descended en masse on Palestine, without some sort of control, the Arabs, already anxious to maintain their hold in this, their greatest possession, would react violently. In order to maintain stability there the British Govt. decided a controlled influx was the only answer, otherwise once the Jews got into Palestine they would simply disappear without trace. It was decided that the Royal Navy would stop the ships carrying the Jews and take them back to holding camps in Haifa, releasing them in controlled batches. Imagine that…you had survived the holocaust, or spent several years hiding from the Nazis in your own country and now suddenly you were to be put within a barbed wire compound until someone decided it was safe to set you

free. As you might expect, there was a strong reaction.
– and following attacks on the boats carrying the Jews,
British ships back at base were attacked by frogmen

"I was on one of the flotilla of 7 destroyers, we
called them the C Hs, because of their names,
Chequers, Chieftain, Chevron etc. The boats we were
shadowing were cattle boats, small run-down
freighters, anything the immigrants thought would be
seaworthy. Whilst out from the shore there were no
restrictions on their movement but as they approached
Palestine, there was a three mile limit off shore. We
had instructions to wait until that boundary was crossed
and then move forward.

"Two destroyers forming a chevron, one either side
of the illegal ship would then close in until they were
trapped between the two Royal Naval vessels. Special
platforms had been erected above the deck of the
destroyers and we young men waited there, padded
from under our chins down to our ankles – this was
because we were warned that women with steel knitting
needles would attack us. First of all, the water hoses
were turned on the occupants packed on the deck in one
solid mass. As they were forced back by the power of
the water, we had to jump and then try to take control
of the ship. Some of these ships had been at sea for
several weeks, babies had been born on them and the
sanitation was absolutely minimal. Everyone, ourselves
included, once back at base, had to be decontaminated
and deloused. It was in fact a very unpleasant
experience which is probably why it has become such
an important part of my Naval memories." Colin put
down his papers and looked around.

"My grandfather is no longer with us but we do
have photographs of his time in the Navy – happy and
sad times. Certainly there are pictures of the boarding
of one of the immigrant ships and one of his favourites,

on which he's written The Calm Blue Waters of the Med., taken on the deck of a destroyer and with the waves rearing up some 7 or 8 feet about the level of the deck. He used to smile when he saw the young wives of servicemen on TV complaining that their men folk had been away from home for two or three months. When he was in the Navy, their periods abroad were always two and a half years. It was on the return from one of these that he met my grandmother, but that's another story......."

As Colin made his way back to where he'd been sitting there was, for a few moments, a stunned silence, then Johann and Rachel were on their feet embracing him.

Good for them! An acknowledgement that however many years have passed since an incident, a blot on a country's behaviour at any time, remains a blot. Sometimes it takes courage to speak out loud and clear and admit that mistakes have been made. Mistakes which must have caused unbelievable heartache and suffering. Judging by the nods of approval, it's clear that everyone here is at one with this. Must say something.

"Thank you Colin, I have never forgotten reading Golda Meyer's autobiography 'My Life', in which she says that in spite of all the protestations from the British Govt. that they were unaware of what was happening in Nazi Germany, they did in fact know about the concentration camps and the ghetto massacres in occupied countries. We have now apologised for our part in the slave trade and the Australians were quick to admit their faults when they learned that the many children sent to their country to be adopted as they'd been promised, the story we heard from Jack, were in fact placed where they just became work horses and, even worse, in situations where they were abused.

"Now, we'll have a short break and then I think Jane's also got something to share with us."

Again, there seemed to be animated discussions and it was some twenty minutes later when Hazel decided to continue.

Jane looks nervous, hope she can do it. Goodness, David has just reached up and given her hand a reassuring squeeze – this is bonding at its best!

An embarrassed cough and Jane began,

"My story is not as exciting as those which have gone before. I was born the middle child of three to hard-working parents who were always resentful of the fact that money was tight and they could not enjoy life in the way they felt they were entitled to. Rarely did they seem happy. My elder sister soon became like them, resentful, and this was for both her and me to worsen when my brother arrived, just 3 years younger than me. Whether our parents saw in him another wage earner I don't know, but from birth he was the apple of their eye and could do no wrong.

"All this sounds like whinging and a betrayal of family life and it is true I built up my own feelings of resentment that I had become the odd one out, undervalued in every way. As an adolescent, I even read books which referred to the 'middle child syndrome' aggravating my feelings even more. My sister fled the nest as soon as she was old enough to leave school. Having passed all her exams she decided university was not for her and, with a friend, set out for London. Amazingly they did find work and any contact we had with her diminished as the weeks went by.

"My brother was clever – clever enough on occasions to burst into artificial tears, complaining that I had twisted his arm, stood on his foot, or any other accusation he could dream up, knowing that this would result in petting and comforting for him and punishment for me. I became a general dogsbody and when not at school, my life was filled with peeling vegetables, hoovering the floors, changing beds – anything which enabled my parents to relax when they returned home, each complaining that they had had a hard day's work.

"My life took on a new and wonderful meaning when I left school and found work in a florist's shop. Now I was surrounded by beauty and, more importantly, by people who loved that beauty. Of course there was hard work involved in the aftermath of sorting and arranging flowers but that was the price to be paid for spending hours amongst such loveliness. The money I earned was handed over to my mother of course, and, if the pocket money I was begrudgingly given was minimal, I was able to cope with that because of the joy I found in my work. This came to an abrupt halt when in his 59th year, my father died of a massive heart attack. My mother already working only part-time because of ill-health, was diagnosed with Multiple Schlerosis which meant she would require permanent assistance in the home. My brother had followed our elder sister's example and ensured he was working and living several counties away when all this happened - which left me.

"Yes, I was distressed to leave the work I loved so much. I had been there for 12 years and was by that time senior assistant to the owner. At just 28 years I took over the running of our home and the full-time care of my mother. I know that many others, sometimes children, have more difficult situations to deal with, but as a young woman, I again felt resentment that my youth was being drained away with little or no feelings of achievement. Without close friends – people fade away when serious illness is involved – the TV became my closest friend, my link with the outside world. I watched with admiration when Susan Boyle suddenly from a life akin to mine, became a world famous star. Sadly I had no similar talents – or none of which I was aware.

"I was in my 34th year when my mother died and I decided it was time to get a grip on myself and make something of my life. After all the scrimping and saving, the house was now paid for and I employed painters and decorators to improve it inside and out. I applied for work at my old florist's and found myself welcomed back. The owner was just about to retire and having severe reservations about putting young assistants in charge. Suddenly I was in a position of authority, from being a nobody, I was a somebody. I took a course in computer operation, ensuring that I could deal with orders and business matters speedily. I encouraged the shop's youngsters to take the course, stressing that on their C.V.s it would be a huge advantage.

"Now, I purchased books on floristry, flower arranging and gardening to broaden my knowledge of the trade. I visited nurseries and talked to their owners about their produce and then took a course in business management and advertising. When my former boss decided to sell the shop I asked for first refusal and after reviewing the shop's accounts my bank agreed to give me a loan.

"On the morning that the papers were signed and I was now the owner, I walked into *my* shop on cloud nine. Looking back I wonder if I was at fault in not prodding myself into action earlier. Had I allowed myself to get into the doldrums too easily and given up on life? Owning the shop meant my life had at last taken an upturn, for which I was and am grateful. My thanks to you all for listening and especially for your support and friendship during the last difficult hours."

The normally pale-faced Jane was flushed with nervousness as she sat down, but again, Hazel noted, there was an encouraging squeeze round her shoulders from David, whilst the others clapped and nodded approvingly.

Well done, Jane. Previously she must have found bonding difficult and now in these unexpected and frightening circumstances she has found it a blessing. She's also found it's not a one-sided matter, but one of give and take. I think from now on she'll be prepared to make more effort to get to know those around her.

***

Chapter 6

"My thanks to you all for being so co-operative. It's 11.15 a.m. and again we have no guarantee as to the actual collection time, so much will depend on the mist which seems to vary almost by the hour. I'm sure you've all seen the order of departure and have all your personal items, jackets etc., ready for the off. There's still plenty of food, so do help yourselves to whatever you need. Those of us leaving last will gather up the palettes etc. and return them to Manuel, we'll try and leave it as tidy as possible for him and there will certainly be ample food to keep him going until the levadas are clear. Once I am back at Reid's I will get all the details about this evening's meal etc., and see that a note is sent to each of your rooms. I will probably ask that we eat at 8.0p.m. to ensure that we all have the opportunity for a bath or shower and a rest in a proper bed – would you all be happy with that?"

Heartfelt cries of 'Oh, please, please'. 'That would be wonderful'.

David was on his feet and held up his hands in a request for silence.

"I don't think we should disperse to the hotel without making two comments. First of all I know you would all want me to thank Hazel for all she has done to make a very difficult situation so much more than tolerable." Murmurs of approval.

"But there's something else we all want to know. You've heard our stories, isn't it time we heard the one from our leader of the pack. What about it, Hazel?"

Laughter all round and a quick, "I'll put that right, back at the hotel," reply. *Just what I can find to talk about, I don't know.*

Looking across the room, Hazel now saw that Manuel had gone behind her whilst she was speaking

90

and was in the bedroom by the corner ottoman, he was signalling and trying to catch her attention. Crossing over she looked at him, slightly puzzled. He had taken from the chest several of the small packages wrapped in tissue which she had seen at its base. He pushed one in her direction and nodded his head to indicate that she should open it. This she did carefully. It was a large handkerchief, a man's handkerchief. Opening it she saw in one corner the embroidered initial J and underneath it the outline of Australia. Her eyes widened and she gasped in disbelief then said out loud, "What on earth…?"

Someone was at her side immediately, taking her arm. It was Jack, "What's wrong?" Wordlessly, she pushed the handkerchief in his direction. His eyes widened and then he laughed and said, "So…she had a relative called Jack, or John, or whatever, and he lives in Australia."

Without replying, Hazel opened the second package Manuel pushed towards her.

Another man's handkerchief this time with an embroidered C and underneath it a tiny but perfect destroyer. No comment this time from Jack, but by now others were drifting in their direction. The third handkerchief was a lady's with the initial M. and the two small masks, smiling and serious, depicting theatricals.

"Good heavens! Who on earth?" This was from David. Next came two handkerchiefs together, A. and an M., with the initials of their charity Medicins Sans Frontieres embroidered underneath; then came Jane's with a J. and tiny bouquet of flowers, David's with a dog, Susan and Gilbert's package with again the amdram masks. By now the whole group was assembled by the bedside turning over the packages, their faces registering complete disbelief at what was in front of them. Below Tom's initial was a small pile of apples and under Sally's a baby's crib and finally Hazel's package revealed a handkerchief with the letter H and in the centre a small, perfect hazel tree with leaves and filberts scattered over the ground. Between the layers of tissue was something else, a sealed envelope. Turning it over she saw the scrawled message…*Please do not open until you are alone.*

Hazel was crying, she didn't know why. Madge and Jane had arms around each other as if supporting each other in shock. The men looked stunned as they turned over the packages, reluctant to meet each other's gaze.

This was surreal, bizarre, unbelievable. How could this lady who had died three weeks ago have known that their group, with these Christian name initials and their own particular threads of memory ingrained were going to be deposited in her home? At what point had she started preparing these gifts? How long had she known that they would arrive? It was uncanny, weird beyond belief. She remembered now, that the policeman had said Manuel's wife was famous for her embroidery and not so popular because of her second sight. Well that figures, if the people who knew her, were like us, overawed by Madeleine's knowledge of things before they happened.

Tears were now rolling down her cheeks and she found herself drawn away from the group, wrapped in Jack's arms, trying to listen to his quiet words of comfort.

"There must be an explanation, but you know none of us can explain everything which happens in this world or know the wonders of the human mind. In any event don't distress yourself. These are all loving messages – messages of good will. That this old lady foresaw our accident, knew we would come here and saw each of us through the stories we told, the stories which *you* asked for, is amazing. But there is no wickedness, no evil here, so we must be grateful for her goodwill. You have been a tower of strength since the accident and you mustn't let go now. Dry your eyes, there's work to be done, I can hear the helicopters. Let's get Sally and Tom and the Williams waiting by the door first of all."

He's so right. Plenty of time to have a weep later.

"Folks, we think the helicopters are about to arrive so Sally and Tom, Sue and Gilbert, make sure you've got your packages and said farewell to Manuel, then please go and wait by the kitchen door. Don't forget your jackets."

Suddenly it was all activity, A flurry of embraces for Manuel and the first four were ready. Within minutes they were airborne and as the first helicopter soared, then dipped out of sight, the second took its place on the promontory.

Those left behind now started a quick attempt at restoring the rooms to some sort of order. Palettes were stacked and carried into the palheiro, the mattresses returned to the bed, food packed away in kitchen cupboards and Manuel shown that there was plenty there for his use.

Hazel was still clutching her small package when Manuel approached her with the remaining parcel from the bottom of the ottoman. It was labelled 'Baby S. and T.' and he thrust it into her hands grinning and motioning that she should take it. Carefully she packed it with her own gift into her small rucksack and motioned that she understood. By the time the first helicopter returned those remaining were ready and they saw the Moreaus and Jane leave. It was time for them to go.

Why did she feel this wave of nostalgia? Throughout there could have been an element of danger, the possibility of another landslip. Initially these were strangers culled together in unusual circumstances, why should she now feel as if something was being taken away from her?

As if reading her thoughts, Jack took her arm and said, "No regrets now, life goes on. You have ensured that what might have been a nightmare, became an acceptable experience, certainly one which none of us will forget. Time to look back with pleasure and pride."

Her confidence boosted, she embraced Manuel, kissing his nut-brown cheeks and said her thanks and the hope that they would meet again. He nodded as if he understood and then bidding them all goodbye went out to wave as the helicopter roared upwards into the blue of the sky.

The pilot had a message for her. Sally had been taken straight to the hospital, as it was suspected that she had started to go into labour. Her husband was with her and all the other travellers were now safely back at Reid's. The Manager there had been informed of Hazel's impending arrival and wanted to talk to her in private. He was in fact waiting for her at the main entrance, shook hands with them all and then ushered Hazel into his study.

"Miss Godwin, I need to talk to you about the traveller who won a great deal of money. I have a message from the donor stating that all Senor Ronaldo's expenses, i.e. the reconstruction of the roof etc., will be paid for. Aware that he wishes to sell the property, the donor suggests it is done as quickly as possible so that he may, as planned, come and live in the village with one of his daughters, but in any event I am told to ensure that he is at no time short of money."

"I'm delighted to hear it. Manuel has been a wonderful host, trying to keep us warm, giving us food and all this, after we had almost wrecked his home.

Once the building work is done he will, hopefully, recoup sufficient money for his needs in the coming years. As a matter of interest, do you actually know the name of the donor?"

"Yes, I do, but I have been asked not to divulge it yet." He smiled, "All will be revealed at your dinner tonight. I have, incidentally, arranged for your party to dine at 8.0 p.m. in the small lounge behind the main dining room – that way you will be completely private. All the members of your party have a note in their rooms to that effect."

"Thank you, you have been most kind."

"Now, I'm sure you will want to go and enjoy being back in civilisation again. Should there be any further news from the hospital, we will keep you informed."

A quick look into the lounge/diner he had mentioned and Hazel saw that all was ready. There were stunning flower arrangements, a Happy New Year notice and balloons over the fireplace, crackers at each place and a general air of festivity. Now she really could go and enjoy a lovely soak in the bath.

**

Hazel's phone rang at 7.40 p.m. just as she was leaving her room to go downstairs.

It was the Manager with the information that Sally's baby had been born and both mother and baby were well. At seven and a half months the baby was below the normal term and the hospital wished to keep mother and baby there for at least another week. Learning that Tom had already returned to Reid's to join the party for dinner, quickly Hazel backtracked into her room to collect the parcel given to her by Manuel, just as the phone rang again. It was Jane asking if there was any news about the baby and congratulating Hazel once again on the way she had handled the most difficult and frightening of situations. Together they exclaimed at the efficiency and goodwill displayed by Reids throughout and their thoughtfulness in providing a separate dining room for this special occasion.

As arranged, the remainder of the group were waiting, in the private dining room, exclaiming about the decorations, delighted with the party atmosphere created and glowing with good humour and relief. Waiters were already pouring out champagne and as Tom entered, right on cue, Hazel spoke. "Friends, we have some good news and here is Tom to convey it. Go ahead Tom."

Embarrassed and proud, Tom grinned at the assembled company and said, "It's great news, Sally and I have a beautiful daughter, born just two hours ago."

There was applause and back slapping and Hazel signalled to the waiters to hand out the champagne.

"Have we a name yet, Tom?"

"Just one so far…Madeleine, we know it's old fashioned but we've always loved it."

Hazel grasped the back of the chair nearest to her. *How many, if any, will remember that Manuel's wife was called Madeleine? Quite a lot, judging by the shockwave of silence, which had suddenly engulfed the room.*

Just as Hazel felt a wave of tension mounting, Jack's strong arm moved to touch her own with the unspoken words, 'Keep cool. Remember what I said.'

There were one or two sharp intakes of breath, then murmurs of approval.

Quickly Hazel intervened, "Right folks, let's drink a toast to welcome Sally and Tom's new baby girl. The toast is Madeleine."

"Now Tom, we have a gift for your new little one."

And with that she handed him the parcel given to her by Manuel. As Tom unwrapped the tissue paper the room suddenly again went still and silent as he held up its contents; a tiny dress in the finest lawn with a matching jacket, exquisitely embroidered with tiny flowers and all in the palest pink. Tom looked puzzled, how could they have got this so quickly, the baby was only two hours old?

"Tom, we can only say that we were asked to pass on this gift to you. Like you we are completely bemused by some of the things which have happened in the last few hours. We can't possibly explain any of them. All I can say is that someone has been watching over us with a mountain of love and for that we must be very, very grateful. Now folks, if you're like me, you are ready for a really good meal and I'm sure that is now on its way."

Without more ado the waiters started serving and Hazel sank back in her chair grateful that she had Tom on her left and Colin on her right. It took her a few moments to absorb just how her group had seated themselves. David she saw was next to Madge and being his usual charming self.

Funny how after a time I found that charm rather irksome. I suppose as a professional, with continuous contact with your customers, the owners of pet animals, that smooth urbane manner becomes a habit, all part of the reassuring process. Madge doesn't seem to mind, perhaps she just lets it flow over her. She's a pretty little thing and probably seven or eight years younger than he is – could be quite a good match for them both. After all he's already told me he can now work as and when he pleases. Good luck to them. The couples all look happy enough. Tom still seems rather stunned and keeps checking his watch as if he feels he should be back at the hospital. Jane is trying to keep him

occupied, but no doubt as soon as the meal's over he'll
be rushing back there again.

Turning to Colin, "We were all intrigued by that chunk of history you told us about, but you didn't say much about yourself. Are you in the Navy?"

Colin smiled, "No, I toyed with the idea and loved hearing my grandfather talk about it, but decided it wasn't for me. I went to Warwick university and read Maths. and Business studies, then took a Chartered Accountancy course. At uni., I met Amy and for a time we seemed happy enough, then she got tired of the fact I always seemed to be working towards yet another exam and that was the end of that. Since then I've been a loner. My work takes me all over the country so it's not ideal for starting any sort of settled existence. Every time I see her my mother wants to know if I've yet met someone – I think she's desperate to have grandchildren."

"I know that feeling!" Hazel grinned. "I decided to make a complete break when I realised that my partner would never accept that I had any capabilities other than cooking him a meal – and *they* never met his high standards. When you realise you're banging your head against a brick wall, it's time to get out."

Jack now intervened, "Pity your ex couldn't see how you handled the last few days, it could have been a lesson well learned."

"Doubt it! He'd still find some excuse for belittling me. I need to talk to you Jack about Australian visits. I know you get a lot of Brits visiting relations, but do you get many organised tours?"

"Of course! Thousands! People come to see Sydney, Melbourne, Perth – all beautiful cities. They come to cross to the Barrier Reef Islands and to see Ayers Rock and the outback. We're very civilised you know – it's not like going to Outer Mongolia. It was through a tour party, coming to play bowls, that my grandfather found he had living relatives. We also now have the cruise ships which do visits as part of their World Tours. Why do you ask?"

"I've only covered the usual touristy places, mainly in Europe, but I think it would be challenging to take a group much further afield."

"Well, if I can be of any help let me know. Take my address and if you can work out something within striking distance of my area it would be great. What about a visit to a farm to see sheep-shearing? We could always organise a genuine English cream tea. But you'd have to visit first, of course, to work out the routes you would take and what to include – again I could help, if you'd let me."

"You've given me some ideas already – thank you. I think they're about to bring in the coffee, so there's something I must say – excuse me." With that Hazel stood up.

"A few hours ago, you all said in no uncertain terms that it was now my turn to get on my feet and tell you a suitable traveller's tale. I've decided it really is time to sing for my supper."

"Until a few years ago my life was fairly ordinary, almost dull. I was fortunate to be born into a happy family with caring parents and a sister just three years older than me. Things changed as soon as my sister was old enough to go out to work. She left home and at times when I really would have welcomed some help, she was never there.

"I married young, too young. Len was training as an accountant and I was working at a travel agent's, 'making the tea' as he constantly reminded me. Once he had qualified he was even more scornful of my lowly status, ignoring the fact that I had passed all my relevant diplomas and often had to go abroad to assess holiday sites. Losing both my parents was the turning point. My sister lived miles away and Len and I no longer had anything in common. I was tired of his constant belittling of the work I did and it was obvious that divorce was the only solution. Once that had been dealt with I asked if I could be considered for a position as a travel guide, which is why I'm here with you today.

"People often ask if any thing unusual has happened on any of my trips – I shall certainly have something to tell them now! I was once asked to escort a party from Cyprus to Cairo on a day's outing. We were met at Cairo Airport by our young female courier, Miriam, who then introduced us to our armed guard for the day. This created a frisson of anxiety. A guard? And armed? Yes, we all now recalled that a few years ago there had been trouble, but surely today wasn't going to be dangerous?

"Traffic in the city was horrendous. Miriam just shrugged this off and said that to the locals, the lines on the roads were ornamental, not to be taken seriously. We saw a flock of sheep at a slip road waiting to cross the main four lane traffic road and a pick-up truck holding a couple of bulls looking not in the least perturbed at having a double decker bus towering over them.

"At last we saw the tops of the Pyramids and the Sphinx. But, quelle horreur! Someone had moved them. Didn't we all know they were way out in the desert? Here, suddenly they were looming above us. O.K. so the city had expanded and swallowed up the desert. Why had no-one told us?

"Once alighted, a horde of teenage boys arrived selling their wares. The boys' patter was bang up to date. "Asda price, buy one, get one free." One of my party, a well-built gentleman was taken aback to receive a pat on the stomach and even more so when the boy with a look of wide-eyed innocence asked, "When is the baby due?" quickly followed by, "Twins?"

"Looking around we saw armed police on foot and on camels. Rides were being offered on other camels, and a friend and I a few seconds later, found an Arab driver standing right in front of us. He was gorgeous! Blonde hair escaping from his turban and the bluest of eyes. Peter O'Toole's Lawrence in the flesh! Bowing low, he extended his hand, saying in perfect English, "Permit me to introduce myself. My name is Moses." We *didn't* laugh, although it was a very close call. We answered equally politely and again declined the offer of a camel ride. Exploding with giggles as we walked away, we agreed it would make a wonderful after-dinner story, which is why you're hearing it now. Meeting Moses at the foot of Pyramids. You couldn't make it up!

"We visited the Tutankhamun exhibition which left us rather saddened, the beauty of what was on display over-shadowed by the fact that to do the artefacts justice, the museum needed at least a million pounds spent on it. Lunch at a five star hotel and even more security. Our own guard seated close by with other guards, all with that give-away pistol bulge in their jacket pockets. Nor was the night-time ride on the ferry to see the magic of illuminated Cairo from the Nile excluded, with a police boat encircling our boat the whole time.

"It proved a long day in which we saw and did a great deal, but for my friend and I the highlight had to be that meeting with Moses."

There was laughter and applause as Hazel sat down. Jack squeezed her hand and with eyebrows raised said, "You're a woman of many talents, in addition to all that administration you make speeches and know how to make the rest of us laugh. Well done!"

"Thanks, Jack. I'm afraid there's another speech on its way. I'll just wait until they've poured any extra coffees, then there's something else I must say." Moments later she stood up.

"Now, I'm afraid I have a confession to make," Hazel looked round the table at the raised eyebrows and surprised expressions. "I have had to tell you quite a lot of fibs and now is the time to put the record straight. It is in connection with our transfer to Reid's when we first arrived. As you know, I told you, and the Reid's staff confirmed it, that the change was made because their sister hotel had unexpectedly to have some repairs made to their premises. Not true, I'm afraid. My travel company, Primetime instructed me to give you that cover story, but told me that in fact one of our group, who wished to remain anonymous, had won a few months ago, a very large sum of money on the European Lottery. The person in question decided it would be nice to give us all a treat by moving us to one of the most famous hotels in the world." Now heads were turning, surveying other individuals as if for the first time. "I don't think any of us have regretted that...?" Murmurs of "Absolutely not".

"Our donor, however, had not bargained on the fact that the elements would make their own decisions about our accommodation and what we would experience in the next few days. I think now is the time for he or she to explain, if not their motives, what, if anything, they feel has been achieved." Hazel sat down amidst gasps of astonishment and waited. Then there were gasps of surprise, followed by silence as Jane stood up and looked around the table, smiling.

"I'm sorry about the deception. I can only say that the root of the problem is that in the few short months since I won an extraordinary amount of money, I've found it can be both a curse and a blessing. As I told you before, I had at last found myself the owner of my florist shop and for the first time, my life was on an even keel. When contacted about the lottery win, I asked from the outset that my name should not be divulged, having read previous horror stories about people in similar circumstances being bombarded with requests for money. I hadn't had a holiday for several years so decided that my first splashing out would be a cruise, something I'd always wanted to do. Deliberately, I did not purchase one of the VIP suites feeling this would be a give-away.

"The cruise programme contained some events for those travelling alone, but at dinner we were seated at table with a mixture of other passengers. That was when I first noticed something disconcerting. Amongst the couples, the wives seemed to keep themselves rather aloof and it took me 24 hours to work out why. They were afraid, not so much that I would steal their husbands, as that their men folk would be expected to provide me with drinks. Once I'd realised that, on the second night before the meal, I said I would be providing the wines that evening. Relief all round and from the wives, smiling faces.

"Two days later I received an invitation to dine at the Captain's table. Just how this happened I never did find out, but clearly, someone, somehow, had learned about the money. After blocking some of the numerous questions from the man seated on my right, it still took me quite a while to realise that he was a journalist out for a story. I was furious – and he didn't get what he wanted. At the end of the meal I thanked the Captain, but explained that having made friends at my original table I hoped he would not be offended if I returned to them the following night. No problem. Until the next night when I found my previous dinner guests rather uptight *again*– obviously intrigued to know why I, of all people, had had such a privileged invitation. With no explanation forthcoming from me, the atmosphere was cool - *again*!

"It seemed it was a case of 'You're damned if you do and damned if you don't'. For several evenings I ate alone in one of the restaurants – not quite the holiday I'd expected. I had already booked a holiday to Madeira before my win, at the Reid's sister hotel. Like many others I'd heard of Reid's and when I asked how many were in my group it occurred to me that I might treat myself and the whole group, without anyone being aware of my involvement. Primetime and Reid's were told to keep the secret; Hazel was told the outline, but until this moment was not aware who was at the heart of it.

"I apologise again for the secrecy, but you can see my dilemma. Knowing about the money seems to affect relationships. What I can say is that you have been the most wonderful of companions. A few days ago we all underwent a traumatic experience and yet, together, we overcame it. Which of us will ever forget the controlled way in which Jack got us off the coach; the way Tom coolly removed the seat and our own medical team extracted the driver and made him comfortable? Under Hazel's excellent guidance we sorted out sleeping arrangements and then like the five loaves and fishes incident we all pooled our resources to ensure we had something to eat. Nor do we any of us overlook Manuel's input. Our language he didn't understand, but our needs he did and made every effort to ensure they were met.

"All of this would have been to no avail if we had just languished for hours waiting to be rescued and losing spirit as the time passed – here again we have

Hazel to thank. The idea of us, like those Canterbury pilgrims, passing that crucial time with personal stories, deepening our relationships as we learned of our origins and attitudes was masterly. Through the stories we got to know each other, we appreciated each other's backgrounds. Knowing the experiences we've each endured and the family stories handed down and valued, enabled us to become closer and to assist us in surviving.

"It also gave me an insight into how many areas my fortune might assist – areas I might otherwise not have considered. So, my friends, sincere apologies for fibbing, thank you for your company and congratulations to one and all. Now I think a toast is long overdue....please stand and raise your glasses. The toast is to Survival, coupled with the name of Hazel Godwin."

And as they stood and raised their glasses, nodding in her direction, the tears once again started to stream down Hazel's face. It was over. Her most dangerous, eventful and successful tour ever!

***

Epilogue

Hazel stretched out in the comfort of her lounger, almost purring with pleasure. The banks of the Swan River were without doubt the most wonderful place in which to relax and drink in the view. The majesty of the river, its breadth, as if the ocean had been brought to her, never failed to amaze. As always, Jack had ensured she had everything she needed. The sunshade was unfurled and he had personally supervised the children as they carefully applied Factor 40 sun cream on themselves and her. Always he was caring, loving and supportive. Her constant thank you to the heavens, *How blessed I am.* Now as she drifted in and out of sleep, she remembered....

First of all, the letter. Read in the privacy of her own room at Reid's, its words burned into her brain, its generosity of spirit staying with her always.

My Dear Hazel,

You will be distressed at first to receive this. The unexpected and the unknown can be very frightening. Shakespeare once said, 'There are more things in heaven and earth, Horatio, than are dreamt of in your philosophy', cling onto that suggestion that humans have only a limited knowledge of our universe. You were wise enough to get your group to introduce themselves through stories, the essence of which reflected their attitudes to life and their backgrounds. Now, I think it only fair that I should do the same.

I was five years old when I realised I was different from other children and, indeed, from other people. I knew that my baby brother was going to die before it happened and that my mother would scald herself in the kitchen. Divulging some of that knowledge to the family, produced such a furore that I started to contain my dreams to myself. Yet somehow I knew they were important, felt that by knowing in advance I could perhaps prevent things happening. There were a few occasions when I was able to do just that. A car, whose brakes had failed, was at my insistence examined and the fault discovered; a woman in pain, was persuaded to go to the hospital, the problem identified as ovarian cancer and cured. Strangely this made me unpopular. What made you weep, made others angry. Many see my second sight as some form of witchcraft, not accepting that I did not wish this upon myself, it was just there.

I was fortunate that my mother was Portuguese and my father, English, so that from my early years I was bi-lingual. I insisted that my daughters also became familiar with the English language. For me, communication was of paramount importance. My marriage to Manuel and the birth of my daughters filled a large part of my life, but not its whole. Often the antagonism from my embroidery successes and from second sight comments which proved to be accurate, were very hurtful, so that I was happier when Manuel and I left the village and went to live on the side of the ravine. There I could concentrate on my embroidery and whilst I was doing that, my dreams. At times, make no mistake, they were frightening. Tragedies I could not prevent happening, plunged me into the depths of depression. For days I knew the 2004 tsunami was about to happen. But who would believe the mad woman who lived in the ravine? I tried to warn the Funchal residents that flooding was imminent some two years ago, but their ears were closed and no precautions were taken. Sadly, people died.

I know that you always when reading this will be shedding tears, but Jack has from the start, encouraged you to turn those from sadness into joy. In those dangerous first hours, I was willing you and your group to live, I was in fact your guardian angel. But it was your resolute behaviour which strengthened those around you and now all will reap the benefit.

My life is coming to its close, whilst for you, life will soon be changed completely because of your journey to Funchal. Love will embrace you as never before and the friendships formed, remain strong for the rest of your life. This, Hazel, has been my story, yours is about to unfold. Savour its pleasures, they are richly deserved. Madeleine Ronaldo.

Hazel opened her eyes with a start. That amazing communication, now safely tucked away in her jewellery box, worn by the many times it had been unfolded and re-read. Only Jack had seen it and discussed with her its precious contents. It was their secret.

Was it really only nine years since they had first met? That dreadful, unforgettable moment as the coach plunged downwards, the panic rising in all of us on board – except Jack. His calm orders encouraging us to move only as and when he said, which certainly ensured our safety. I suppose I knew then he was special. Now, daily, I am reminded of it.

We both went through the motions of making excuses to see each other again.

We discussed a visit with a touring party which he and I knew was never going to happen. We like to think it was an instinctive ruse on both our parts to make sure our deepening affection and need for each other

108

would blossom. Within a few months of that meeting we were married and I was installed in Jack's large, rambling farmhouse. The vastness of the land he owns never ceases to amaze me, nor does his ingenuity. The large vegetable garden is carefully irrigated, the flower garden automatically watered daily and our home planned to the last detail with the long veranda sited to catch the late afternoon and evening sun, but offering protection from the ferocity of Australia's blistering mid-days. Strangely enough, we did follow up on some of those early, quickly dismissed, way-out ideas and the sheep-shearing visits followed by an English cream tea have paid dividends, with contacts from all over the world enriching both our lives.

Hard to believe that our boys are now six years. My shock at learning I was carrying twins was in complete contrast to Jack's calm acceptance of the knowledge, as he smilingly reminded me, that he was quite accustomed to delivering twins and triplets at lambing time. His thoughtfulness is applied to all situations. Already he has made it clear that there must be no pressure for the boys to follow in his footsteps. We must express equal delight should they decide to go to university and follow a completely different course. Always he insists, "As individuals we must plough our own furrow; work which you love and understand is a strong basis for a happy life." Like me, he hopes that the child I'm carrying now is a girl. We agree that it would provide our boys with a balanced family home and, Jack insists, she must have dark auburn hair and hazel eyes, just like her mother!

Typically, he's taken the children into town for an hour or so, to enable me to rest for a while. Yes, I am resting, but my mind constantly remembers...

Leaving Madeira...Each of us visiting Sally in hospital and meeting the new baby, exclaiming at her perfection; the decision to hold the christening in the hospital chapel so that all of us might be present; the request for Jane, Jack and me to be godparents and our surprise on learning the baby's Christian names would be Madeleine Reid; the Manager's enthusiasm on being told this and his prompt registration of the baby as the hotel's first Honorary Life Member. It all seemed so perfect and if we rarely discussed it, we none of us forgot Madeleine Ronaldo who had somehow anticipated everything and showered us with blessings. I wasn't surprised when David and Madge married. Theirs was a lovely wedding in a small Suffolk village. Jack had already gone back to Australia, but the Landaus, the Williams and Moreaus were all present and Jane and Colin, of course.

Jane had some news for me. She had already expressed concern about how best to handle her large sum of money. From the start the Lottery company had dealt with it, but she felt that was not sensible as a permanent arrangement. Learning of Colin's background in finance she'd asked my advice as to whether she should ask him to take over. I could only say that I felt he was totally reliable and so the deal was settled. He'd resigned from his current work and become her official accountant and financial advisor. For a year they managed with him living a hundred miles away, but Jane had by that time bought a lovely old house in the West Country which had two cottages on its estate. Her suggestion that he moved into one of these was met with alacrity and so their own association and respect for each other deepened. At the wedding of David and Madge she told me that she and Colin were also making plans to marry – adding 'You wouldn't believe the lengths he's going to, pre-nuptial contracts etc., etc. to ensure that should anything go wrong he will not be the recipient of my money!'

Jane's own generosity continues unabated – first it was thousands to the Médicins Sans Frontières, the charity where the Moreaus worked. Having heard their concerns for the children orphaned by national disasters, Jane set up a new charity to ensure as many of these children as possible were safely housed and cared for. Just six years since have now elapsed since the Moreaus fulfilled their dream and adopted a brother and sister and their joy in their family shines through their letters. A vast amount of money has gone to the arts to ensure people like Sue, Gilbert and Madge are not starved of their love of both amateur and professional theatre, with contributions to those who provide sanctuary for animals. Nor have Sally and Tom been omitted from Jane's list of beneficiaries. Baby Madeleine has had a Trust Fund opened in her name and as Jane is her godmother she insisted, in spite of their protests, that Tom and Sally should have a larger house – one with four bedrooms to allow for any other additions to the family. The Landaus too received a generous donation enabling them to locate small Jewish communities, descendants of the holocaust survivors, who were still struggling and, wherever it was needed, funds were provided.

To me, Jane has been a wonderful friend – giving me wise counsel about uprooting and moving to another country, promising faithfully that she and Colin will visit us next year. She now has a chain of florist shops in the South West and I'm happy that she has the pleasure of overseeing her beloved flowers which give joy to others. Always she expresses her thanks for my Pilgrims' Tales, assuring me that the bonding with members of our group, all knowing nothing about her money, provided for her the watershed following its receipt; a watershed which enabled her to go forward and spend it wisely.

I'm grateful for everything I now hold dear, a loving husband, our beautiful children and our friends, so many friends, new and old. Always I give thanks for my guardian angel, Madeleine, who was watching over me and my travellers, all those years ago. This particular traveller has already many more wonderful tales to tell!

Deo Gratias.

***

www.ingramcontent.com/pod-product-compliance
Lightning Source LLC
Chambersburg PA
CBHW030133260626
47156CB00008B/2933